I0748241

Visit the author's website at www.ladyofkaos.com

NESA MILLER

# Contents

# ANGEL AND SID

A singular monolithic beast loomed ahead. Quite an unexpected sight in the middle of the pink and purple patchwork of the moors. Etain breathed in the crisp autumn air, a creepy tingle crawling over her scalp as she stared at the rectangular structure. "Where are we going?"

The silver-haired man turned. A toothy grin appeared within the bush of his silver beard. "Just ahead."

*What's his name? Sid? Yeah. Sid. And she's...Angel.*

She adjusted the pack on her shoulder and nodded toward the building. "You expect me to go in there with you? Or is this a drop and run kind of scheme?"

Sid gave his partner a steely-eyed glare. Angel silenced him with a raised hand and approached Etain. "I know it looks a bit scary—"

Her gaze slid to the blond woman dressed in blue leather armor. "I'm not scared of the *stupid* building. It's what happens once I walk through the doors."

Angel stood straight as a board. "Life is what goes on in there. It's where we live."

"You'll probably say anything to get me inside—"

Sid threw his hands into the air, eyes bugging out of his head. "I've better things to do. We didn't have to come after you, ya ungrateful little heathen. If G weren't so insistent on saving your ass, I'd of left ya to the wolves."

Her ears perked up at the mention of the man. "G? Vivian said the name, too. Is he in there, waiting to force me into whatever it is you people do?"

Sid huffed again.

Angel eyed the girl. "G is the chieftain of our clan. Remember me telling you we're with Darth? Didn't Vivian mention it?"

Etain shrugged, her attention more on the beast of a building than on the conversation. "Probably."

A whirlwind blasted through the front doors, headed straight toward Etain. She slipped the pack from her shoulder and gripped the hilt of her sword. A bald brickhouse of a man with a heated glare she was sure would melt steel stood before her. "I'm usually more diplomatic and give newbs the option of walking in of their own free will. But you seem to be either too stubborn or ignorant—"

*Well, if the glare doesn't do it, the gravel voice will.*

Angel shook her head. "Oh, G, she's not ignorant—"

"Quiet, Angel," he barked over his shoulder, his green-blue eyes on Etain.

Given a closer view of the man, she noticed he wasn't bald but had sandy blond hair cropped close to his scalp. And not a brickhouse. *More like a Freightliner.*

"Then stubborn it is." He ducked in a linebacker stance, shoved into her mid-drift, causing her to lose her pack and sword, and tossed her over his shoulder.

Etain twisted and turned. "Put me down! I've heard about people like you." And tried to land a good kick anywhere she could but the man clamped one muscular arm over her backside and the other around her legs.

"Sid, bring her pack." G whirled and stalked toward the doors. "Angel, you come with me so *Little Miss* doesn't waste her energy worrying about *stupid* things like her virtue."

Etain stopped struggling long enough to push the hair from her face and glared at Sid with his shit eating grin. "You people are gonna pay for this."

Sid laughed. "Ooooh. I got goosebumps up and down my arms."

"Since daddy's come to save your ass," she quipped.

G stepped hard, giving her a good jolt. "Zip it."

It knocked the wind out of her but the frown on Sid's face made it worthwhile.

Once inside, the shuffling of feet and the scrape of heavy doors as they closed didn't bother her much. She'd find her way back later and slip out. Her heart ramped into overdrive when the turning of multiple locks rang in her ears. *Not good.* Tremors ran through her, turning her stomach.

"Settle down," he ordered.

She pushed and twisted against the big man, lifted the tail of his shirt, and...

"Ow!" he roared.

In the next moment, she hit the floor, the cloak over her head.

"She bit me!"

Angel rushed to his side. "Yep, it's a good one, too. Someone get the first aid kit. Hurry!"

Etain pushed off the cloak and sat up, blood trickling down her chin. Her gaze moved from person to person as she stood, rubbing the shoulder she'd landed on. With everyone distracted by the cry-baby master, she spied her pack next to Sid and dashed past him, slung it onto her shoulder and slipped through another doorway.

A long row of doors stood open, each room spilling into the next, the first one blue, the next white, transitioning into red, and yellow, and orange, and black. No one chased after her, no one moved toward her. They merely watched in fascination.

Eventually, at the end of the torrential onslaught of rooms, she came to a wide curved staircase. *Going up isn't gonna get me out of here.* She shifted her pack and veered around the stairs.

There it was. Beckoning to her. A serious door made all the more intimidating by the bands of rivets crisscrossed over its metal skin. *This is the time to be brave. You're Alamir after all.*

The cool yet formidable handle turned easy enough—over and over and over again.

"Goddamn it." She pressed her forehead to the metal barrier, the coolness of the façade easing the ache in her head.

*No one will ever know what happened to me.* A tear rolled down her cheek. "I'm sorry, Daddy."

The hair on the back of her neck rose. She closed her eyes and exhaled.

"Don't be sorry, yet. You've only just arrived."

She turned to the oaf who had dragged her here, her fingers wrapping around the hilt of her sword while slipping the backpack down into her other hand. Her blade met his, deflecting his advance, followed by a bushwhack to his head with her pack. He staggered but stayed on his feet. Etain released the pack, pivoted, and lunged for the kill.

The big man blocked her move and landed a well-placed kick to her midsection, doubling her over and back into the metal door. With a loud, "Oof," she crumpled, her sword clanging on the stone floor.

*That hurts.* She sucked in a breath. "Great plan, there. *Master G*," she wheezed through gritted teeth. "You get your jollies by man-handling girls?"

He loomed over her with Angel and Sid behind him. "Leave yourself open. Get your ass kicked."

At least he had the decency to offer her a hand as if she would accept. She licked her lips, impaling the man with a glare, pushed against the wall, and struggled to her feet. With one arm around her mid-drift, she carefully retrieved her sword.

G sheathed his blade. "You're Alamir. Girl. Time to fight like one."

She wheezed another breath. "I don't know which—I'm more tired of—people wanting to fight me—or the ones—wanting to teach me—how to fight."

Angel bustled past G. "Leave her be now. She's had enough and you've seen enough." She wrapped an arm around Etain. "Come on, let's get you cleaned up and settled in your room. Sid, get her pack and meet us upstairs."

Etain leaned against the woman for a moment, catching her breath. "No. I'll get it."

"No. You won't." Angel held onto her with an iron grip. "Sid! Get a move on. We have a fair flight of stairs to hobble up."

"Yes, ma'am, Ms. Bossy Boots. I'm right behind ya."

Etain sat on the edge of the bed, her sword still in her hand and watched the two move around the room, checking for what, she wasn't sure. There wasn't much—bed, side table, desk, chair, and closet. Pretty stripped down compared to the one at Vivian's but at least she had a window and her own space *Hopefully.*

Angel stood in front of her. "It isn't much but it's clean and you're safe. There's a shower room and toilet down the hall. Most of what you'll need should be in the closet just outside it."

Sid set her pack on the bed beside her. "Little lady, you get some rest, and we'll catch up at supper." He kissed his lady on the cheek. "I'll see ya downstairs, babe."

Etain waited until he closed the door. "Am I a prisoner?"

Angel sighed and sat next to her. "Honey, you aren't a prisoner."

"But I can't leave. Right?"

"Do you have somewhere you need to be?"

Etain glanced at her from the corner of her eye. "I don't need to be here."

Angel slapped her hands on her knees and shrugged. "Well, you don't know anything about here, do you? So let's give it a minute before you make a final decision. From my point of view," she stood and faced her, "all you have outside of this place is trouble. Get yourself cleaned up and come down for supper. Meet the clan."

Etain grabbed her pack and slid her blade into its sheath. "I need to pee."

Angel shook her head and walked to the door. Standing in the doorway, she pointed down the hall. "Bathroom is that way. Everything you need—"

"Is just outside. I heard you."

She pressed her lips together, nodded, and quietly closed the door.

Etain looked around the room, wrapped her arms around herself, and curled into a ball on the bed.

⁂

Angel plodded down the stairs aware G expected her in his office, but she had so many other things she'd rather do. Like find Sid and go for a long walk or meet Winston in the kitchen for a cooking lesson or even go back upstairs and give that poor, lonely girl a motherly hug. *I'm sorry for whatever brought you to us. I could tell by the look in your eyes it was beyond your understanding.*

She found herself at the door of the office but turned away. G and his insane third eye perception called her name as though he saw her through the door. "Angel, come in."

She closed her eyes and turned the knob. Inside, Sid sat in one of the chairs in front of the desk, the other waiting for her.

G stood, ice pack to his right eye, and motioned to the empty chair. "Thank you for joining us."

Protocol called for the invited to be seated and quietly wait for G's permission to speak. But for Angel, this day she chose to ignore it. "I don't condone what went on earlier. Have you lost your mind?" She stalked toward the desk. "She's just a girl, G. You might not see it, but I do. What you did wasn't right."

G considered her for a moment, glanced at Sid, and shrugged. "You can damn me all you want. She isn't going to show me anything by being nice. Hell, I doubt she has control over it." He came from behind his desk. "Until I see it for myself, I can't help her."

She trembled but would not let anger get the upper hand. "Damning you is the least of my wishes. I can only hope when she shows you her true power, it knocks you on your ass into next year."

"Angel. I'm sorry you're upset." A deep frown creased his brow as he approached. "Her reactions told me plenty." He bowed his head but held her gaze. "Please remember, we're dealing with an unknown here."

She crossed her arms over her chest. "How about giving her time to take it in? No one can get to her while she's here."

"We may not have the luxury."

"And pushing her isn't gonna end well for any of us."

Sid came out of his seat. "G, give us a few days to work with her, make her comfortable, and a chance to meet the clan. She has a wild streak but she's smart."

He turned to his second in command. "Wild I can handle. The girl isn't afraid to fight." G swiped a hand across his near bald head. "The challenge is the intelligent part."

Sometime during the night, an urgent need to pee woke Etain. She uncurled her body in the dark room and lay on her back, sorting the where and when in her mind. "Fuck. What the hell am I gonna do?" She pushed up, her booted feet landing on the floor and stood. "How about we pee?"

"Excellent idea, *little miss*." She grabbed her pack, waiting until her eyes adjusted to the darkness, and made her way to the door. Quietly, she opened to a dimly lit hallway, looking one way and the other, and headed toward the bathroom on light feet. She dashed into the first toilet stall she came to, dropped her pack, unzipped her jeans, and rolled her eyes closed from the heavenly release. "Ha-le-lu-jah."

Dressed and no longer distracted by nature, she stepped from the gray stall and washed her hands, eyeing herself in the wall-to-wall mirror. "You look like hell. But. I don't care." She leaned over the sink and slammed the mirror with her wet hands, "Maybe they'll keep their distance until I can find a way out," leaving two watery marks dribbling to the white stone countertop.

In the absence of a towel, paper or otherwise, she wiped her hands on her jeans and returned to the stall for her pack, slinging it onto her shoulder. "Let's find something to eat."

Quiet accompanied her down the long, gray hallway. She stopped occasionally, pressing her ear to a door and waiting for a voice or a noise, anything, to give her some form of information about the people around her. *I know they're here. I saw them downstairs.*

At the next door, she turned the handle. *Locked.* And crossed the hall to the next door. *Locked.* As was every door, except hers. *Is this how clans work? Secrets locked away? Or are they afraid of me?* She ran a hand through her hair. *Why not lock me in instead of out?*

At the top of the stairs, she glanced over her shoulder. "Cower in your crappy little rooms. I'm outta here."

Step after step, she descended, stopping every so often and peering down the dark stairwell. Much like the hallway she'd left behind, a dim light shown at the bottom beckoning to her and so she continued until her labored breathing made it impossible to go on. *What the hell? It didn't take this long to get to the room.* She glanced over the banister again. The dim light appeared as far away as it had earlier.

Etain veered from the stairs at the next floor, walked the hallway and compared it to where she'd come from. It looked the same, but most buildings worked like this. *Right? Nothing unique. No imagination in design. Just floor on floor of door after door.* "Are they all locked?"

She pressed her ear to the first one. *Nothing.* The cool handle warmed at her touch. When it clicked and the door opened into darkness, her heart quickened, ears piqued for the sound of a footstep, a breath, or a voice challenging her presence.

Silence, except for her own breathing, invited her into the room. The décor was no different—bed, side table, desk, chair—and neither was the floor plan. Even the window was in the same spot.

The crazy, creepy tingle crawled along her spine and over her scalp.

She pivoted toward the bed. The covers were rumpled as though someone had curled up on top of them. "No."

Out of the room in seconds, she ran toward the door at the end of the hallway with no regard for the echoes of her boots against the stone floor, and crashed into the toilet with its multiple stalls, slamming the door against the wall. This time, she noticed how the lights automatically flickered to life. She turned to the wall-to-wall mirror, marred by two dripping handprints. "Holy crap!"

Not yet convinced, she dashed back to the stairs and flew down several flights, exiting onto another floor. The bedroom was the same, crumpled covers included, as was the dimly lit hallway, and the ridiculous toilet with its multiple stalls.

"Mother fucker," she whispered and threw her pack at the handprints on the wall-to-wall mirror, smashing them into pieces.

With her pack slung over her shoulder, she went floor to floor, making sure she added a new level of damage to not only the toilet but the bedroom as well. Each subsequent floor reflected the exact same.

After hours of destruction, she dropped on the landing of a floor she'd become quite familiar with, albeit unsure of which one.

# THE LIBRARY

The smoky smell of a campfire made her smile as she walked into the kitchen, mom at the stove, a cast iron skillet in front of her and a set of tongs in her hand, wisps of smoke curling around her head like a morning fog.

Her mouth watered at the symphony of pops and crackles anticipating the moment when her teeth crunched into a salty, savory delight.

Dad stood next to mom with his own pan, swishing hot oil over the eggs enough to encase the yolks in a delicate film of yummy juiciness, the two laughing like kids at play instead of parents preparing a sumptuous breakfast for the family.

Etain laughed, sitting at the table. "Do y'all always have this much fun?"

As her parents turned, her dad split in two at the waist and mom slid apart in pieces.

"No!" she screamed, extending a hand but unable to get to them. Their blood splashed across the room drenching her from head to toe. She fell onto the floor, watching the light fade from their eyes through her tears.

Hand over her heart, its rhythm rumbling like a Harley, her eyes popped open, darting left and right. A campfire smell hung in the air but there was no blood, no kitchen, no mom or dad. The tears fell, though, crying for what she'd lost and the hunger gnawing at her insides.

The night had passed with her on the landing, curled in a tight ball. "Damn." With a swipe of her eyes, she sat up, "Bacon," pushed to her feet and grabbed her pack. "God knows how long this is gonna take." A peek over the banister had her rolling her eyes. She was on the ground floor within a couple of turns. "Asshole."

The sweet, smoky fragrance led her to its source where an unassuming man stood at an oversized range directing others with a wave of his tongs. "Let's get these people fed. We have souls to save and new Alamir to find."

He turned at her entrance and raised a brow. "Speaking of new souls, come in young lady." His Canadian accent reminded her of a client who'd worked with her father. "I'm Winston. Who are you?"

Etain relaxed when he smiled. "Uh, I-I'm Etain. Nice to meet you."

"Welcome to Darth, Etain. If you'll shuffle into the room next door, you can grab some breakfast. And make sure you eat all of it. Depending on the day, you might not get another chance."

"Oh, okay." An approaching tray of food had her scooting into a corner. "Sorry."

Winston's eyes twinkled. "Terry! Slow it down, man!" He winked at Etain. "Always in a hurry."

Left to fend for herself, she followed the tray into a room filled with people but held back at the door and gawked at the unfamiliar faces. No Sid or Angel. Not even the asshole was present.

A mix of giggling young women and men came through the door.

*I'm not fourteen anymore. I doubt they'll see me as any different from them.* She secured her pack on her shoulder, fell in step with the group and mimicked their moves, taking a plate and moving from serving tray to serving tray. A person at the end of the table shoved a fork and knife into her hand and pointed her toward rows of tables across the large room.

Although no one seemed to take notice of her, bottoms shuffled at her approach closing gaps between them. Without so much as a glance at the rude miscreants, Etain veered toward a different table close to the floor to ceiling windows along the outer wall.

She sat across from a girl with long dark hair, creamy complexion, and big blue eyes. "You must be the most talented one here."

In mid-bite of a biscuit, the girl stared at her with knitted brows. "Why?"

Etain shoved her pack under the table between her legs and picked up the fork, eyeing the food on her plate. "They look like the type who think they have talent and can't stand those who actually do." She met the gaze of the other girl as she shoved a forkful of eggs into her mouth.

The girl laughed, covering her mouth with her hand as she chewed the bit of biscuit. "Sorry. I doubt they even notice me. I'm Roxy."

"They notice you. It's why you're sitting here by yourself."

"But I'm not by myself, am I?" Roxy bit off another piece of biscuit.

Etain smiled. "How long have you been here?"

"Long enough to have my own fan club." She indicated the tight asses with a flick of her eyes. "A few weeks."

Etain chuckled. "Where were you before this?"

"Scotland. G and his team found me and brought me here."

"Huh. G. Is he the master of the house?"

Roxy shrugged. "In a way. Some consider him a master at what he does."

She waved her fork with a twist of her wrist. "Which is?"

"Different things. Mostly he takes in newbies and teaches them how to be Alamir."

"There seems to be a lot of that going around." Etain ripped a biscuit in half and bit off a corner. "Any idea on how to get out of here?" Her gaze flicked to the row of windows where light poured in but didn't offer a view.

Roxy leaned forward and lowered her voice. "You won't be going anywhere for a while. We're in lockdown."

The creepy tingle from the previous night crawled along her spine. "Why?"

The girl shrugged and stood. "The word is they brought in someone new last night. Someone dangerous."

*Must've been after me.* "Dangerous?"

She nodded as she picked up her dishes. "G had a helluva black eye this morning."

Etain grinned. "Really?"

"Oh, aye. By the scowl on his face, I'd say he's not had many of those." She winked as she left the table.

Etain twisted in her seat. "Where you going?"

"Training."

"Can I come with?"

Roxy stopped and looked down at her. "Haven't you a teacher?"

Etain shook her head. "No. I just came in last night."

The color drained from her face and the dishes on her tray clinked. "Oh. Well. I-I'm sure they'll get someone... I've got to go."

Etain watched her scuttle away, drop off her dishes at the door, and detour back toward the table of assholes. After sharing a few words with a snooty, long-haired redhead, all eyes turned to Etain. *It's like that, is it?* She met the gaze of as many as she could without losing her breakfast, slung her pack onto her shoulder, stood and walked out of the dining hall.

*Great. Where do I go? If I'm so special they drag me here, where's Sid and Angel? Better yet, where's this Master G.* She laughed as she walked along the corridor and turned at the stairs.

There they were. The rooms attached one to another—their colors melding into the next. *That's the way to the front door.* She bit her bottom lip. *What're the odds?*

The sound of feet shuffling in her direction set her in motion, moving through the colorful rooms but in the opposite direction.

"Hey, girl!"

"Silver hair! Wait up!"

She glanced over her shoulder. Sure enough, the hoard followed, the redhead in the lead. Etain turned away. In front of her another hoard coming from the opposite direction presented an advantageous opportunity. Their numbers offered the perfect cover as she steered through the middle traversing the colors, room after room, and breezed into the foyer, past the front door into new territory.

At a carved wooden door, she glanced behind her again and grimaced at the sea of bobbing heads. *This is as good as any.* She ducked into the room behind the door, dashed into the shadows at the back, and held her breath, listening for sounds of pursuit.

After several eternal minutes, she released the breath and leaned her head against the wall. *Not today, Satan. Probably tomorrow, but not today.*

She turned to shelves and shelves of books from floor to ceiling. Old books faded and well used, many with frayed spines, their titles barely readable. Her fingers gently danced along the promised hours of distraction. Warfare, swordsmanship, strategy, several teased of various styles of martial arts—a practice she was keen to learn—psychology, body language, sex, and so many other topics. *It could take weeks.*

Many touted of meditation while others hinted at types of religions. *Religions?* She opened one such book and thumbed through its worn pages. Its slightly sweet, woody aroma reminded her of the old books in her dad's library. Monotheism, polytheism, henotheism, so many *-isms* she reverently closed the book and returned it to its spot on the shelf. *Dad never mentioned religion.*

Although rows and rows of books filled the room, it wasn't a huge library but enough she could perhaps go unnoticed. And maybe *Master* G wouldn't find her either.

⁕

Toward the end of her first day in the library, Etain waited until the hallways were clear to venture from her sanctuary and headed in the direction of the multicolored rooms. Upon hearing voices, she turned and went back the way she'd come, past the foyer and the library, deeper into unknown territory.

Purely by chance, she discovered another stairway behind a random door. Where the first set of stairs rambled upward to a multitude of floors, this one went up one floor and no further. The elaborate metal railing and balustrade surprised her. *Pretty fancy work for a back stair.* Hand on the rail, the squeak of her boot's rubber sole echoed in the stairwell.

She held her breath, her grip tight on the railing. No voices spoke, no doors opened. She carried on to the next level where, sure enough, a door opened onto a familiar floor. Since nothing distinguished this door from the others, she didn't feel quite so silly for not noticing it last night. In no particular hurry, she walked to the other end where the sight of a door, hanging at a wonky angle on the jamb, confirmed she was on her floor.

Just to be sure, she peeked inside and couldn't help but grin as a sense of accomplishment bloomed in her chest. *Yep. It's almost like a secret passage.*

At the growl from her stomach, she closed the door, *here's hoping the dinner rush is over,* and glided down the closest stairs in search of a quick meal. No one showed as she approached the dining hall.

She bit her bottom lip and shifted her pack. *They're either done or sitting in there stuffing their faces.* She ventured closer and peeked inside.

The serving dishes were on the table, their little burners blazing away, and a few stragglers in various stages of devouring their food. *No one I recognize.* Her ears piqued for the slightest note of someone's approach, she partially filled a plate, and sat at the same table, her eyes on the move as she too devoured her food. *Nice work, Winston. I gotta remember to thank you next time I see you.*

Etain stacked her dirty dishes on top of the others and returned to her room for what she hoped would be a good night's sleep. *Maybe Angel or Sid will be around tomorrow and show me where I should be.*

Several days passed much in the same manner—up early, pee, brush her teeth, grin at the mess she'd become and the mess she'd made, sit in the library for early morning reading, circle back upstairs to avoid the multicolored rooms, and grab a quick breakfast after the others were gone, back upstairs and down the other side to the library for more reading and practice. No one came looking for her. No Sid. No Angel. No Master G. And oddly enough, no librarian. No overheard conversations mentioned the "silver-haired girl." The longer she didn't exist, the deeper she delved into her books.

On a few occasions, a person or two entered the library but never stayed long. The first time it happened, she scrambled from her chair and stood in a dark corner, holding her breath, watching as they took a few steps, stopped, turned, and left.

After a week, and having become accustomed to the occasional visitor, she positioned a chair in the dark corner where she could read at her leisure and keep an eye on the comings and goings. As time went by, those who utilized the library began to stay longer but kept to the front. No one ventured toward the back.

After a couple of more weeks, as she practiced with her sword, a young man interrupted her routine. "Excuse me."

She stopped, eyes wide, lowered her sword and slowly turned to a shaggy headed blond with eyes as blue as the sea, tall and handsome. "Yes?"

"What're you doing?"

"I'm, uh, practicing. With my sword." She held it up in case he hadn't seen it.

"In the library?"

"This is where the books are." She waved a hand toward a stack on the floor.

His beautiful blue eyes flicked down but came back to her. "Is that where you learned what you were doing?"

"I'm sorry. Who are you?"

The smile on his face lit the room. "Tristan. Sorry. And you are?"

She stuck out a hand. "Etain. Nice to meet you." He raised an amused brow but accepted. *He has the cutest little dimple when he smiles.*

"Will you teach me?"

"Well, I've only just started on it."

"Can we learn together?"

She shrugged. "Sure. Do you have your—"

"Always." Tristan drew his sword from the scabbard across his back.

Etain smirked. "Okay. Cool. Put your big boy away for now. There isn't enough room for both of us in here and it'd be better if we had a mirror." At his raised brow, she added, "So you can check your form." She rested a finger over her lips. "I think I know just the place. Come with me."

She led the way taking the hidden stairs to the second floor and into the toilet. At the doubtful expression on his face, she chuckled. "You'll see."

"What happened to the mirror?"

"Don't worry about it. You stand over here where it's not broken." She lifted her sword. "Take your stance. One foot back and the other forward. Find your balance. Good. So with a sword like this, we're gonna hold the hilt with both hands for a thrust and lunge."

They worked together for part of the morning until Tristan had another class. "Thanks, Etain. Same time tomorrow?"

"Yeah. Sure. I'll meet you here."

While Tristan went his way, Etain returned to the library. Maybe she could find another move to add to the thrust and lunge.

Settled in her dark corner, a young couple entered the room, peering over their shoulders. One turned down the lights while the other shoved books from the sofa set just inside the door. Etain quietly closed her book and waited, her eyes on the couple.

Once both were on the sofa, even with her limited experience, she soon understood their intent. The kissing and the groping she expected. *Not like in the movies but, hey, we aren't movie stars here.* When clothes came off and body parts exposed, rather than scandalized at their nudity, she found the clumsiness of their moves appalling. *Certainly not Collins worthy.*

Etain pushed from the chair, grabbed her pack, and walked a couple of rows down, searching for the book she'd read yesterday. *Ah. There you are.* Taking it from the shelf, she spied another in her stroll toward the grunting, pumping couple, and added it to the first one. Coming closer, she almost turned and disappeared into the shadows at the young man's face twisted in what she assumed was sexual pleasure, but his dark eyes popped open and looked straight at her.

Her heart skipped unsure of whether to be embarrassed or intrigued until she understood his glare as arrogance instead of surprise. It snapped her right out of little girl mode. She shifted to one hip, smirked, and dropped the books on the floor next to him. "If you're gonna do it, at least make it interesting. If you can't read, the big one has pictures. For the sake of your partner, I hope you *can* because the little one tells in *great detail* how it works. The panting, the moaning, all of it. You won't have any trouble finding the right pages. It seems to be popular." With a flick of her hair, she sauntered to the door, turned up the lights, and left the room.

# BANTER AND REPARTEE

Dressed in riding leathers, Sid and Angel trailed behind their latest acquisitions rescued from along the western coast of England and into Scotland. "Do you think she's found her way?"

Sid held the door for his lady. "We've been gone for weeks. I figure she's taken over the place by now."

Angel chuckled as she stepped inside, removing her gloves, and tucking them into her waistband. "Wouldn't surprise me one bit."

"Welcome back," G said, coming down the winding stairway. "How'd it go?"

Sid glanced at his wife and shrugged. "About the same as usual. We found five of 'em. Couldn't locate the other two."

G crossed his arms over his chest and stroked his chin. "Well, that's not good. No idea where they went?"

Sid clasped his hands behind his back. "Nope. And no one recognized our descriptions either. Are you sure they transitioned?"

"My source has been reliable so far, but I guess no one's perfect. Eh?" The chieftain dropped his arms and turned to Angel. "I can tell you're itching to ask me something. Spit it out."

She raised a brow. "How's Etain? Has she settled in?"

"Hmph." He about faced and walked from the room.

"G," she called out. "*Where's* Etain?"

At the doorway, the big man stopped, inhaled, and faced her. "I've only just returned myself. A situation of utmost urgency came about and had to be dealt with."

Her jaw dropped. "You were supposed to be training her." She briefly closed her eyes, shaking her head, and breezed past him. "Heaven help me. We trusted you to watch over her."

G turned as she passed. "Where do you think you're going? You have a report—"

She whirled with fire in her eyes. "Sid has your report. I have better things to do."

Sid pressed his lips together and followed after his wife. "You got everything I know. We best get to looking for her."

Angel headed through the multicolored rooms to the back stairs toward Etain's room. At the wonky door hanging partly open, she stopped and stared, not sure whether to knock, storm through, or leave it for later. "Etain?" When no response came, she gently pushed through the door. "Etain? It's Angel. Are you here?"

Her breath caught in her throat at the state of the room. "What on earth?" Sheets covered the floor with the mattress on the other side of the room. The desk hung out the broken window and the chair was nothing more than splinters. Angel sensed her husband behind her and leaned against him. "Sid," she whispered, "Do you think someone here—"

His arms went around her waist. "Not for a second. This looks more like a temper tantrum."

G showed at the door as she asked, "Why? What would've set her off?"

"That would probably be me," he said coming into the room.

Angel pulled away from her husband's arms. "What did you do?"

"Just a little sleight of hand." At her thin-lipped expression, he added, "To keep her occupied."

She set her hands on her hips. "Some of your mumbo jumbo garbage?"

"Well, I admit, I wasn't expecting this."

"I didn't like leaving her in the first place. If I'd known you were going to torture her," she headed toward the door, "I would've told you to shove your assignment up your—"

G furrowed his brows. "Where you going?"

"To check the rest of the floor. Whatever mess there is will need to be cleared."

He followed her and Sid. "*She* can damn well do the cleaning."

Angel stopped. "She will not. This is *your* mess. *You* fix it." She pivoted on her heel and stalked straight to the only other room the girl had access to. What she found on the other side of the door brought her to a standstill, covering her mouth with her hand. Sid ran into her.

G slowed his approach. "Is it destroyed?" He stood beside the couple and gawked the same as them.

Lined in formation, swords in hand, a group lunged at the shattered mirror, stepped back, pivoted, and lunged again.

"Much better!" Etain clapped her hands and stepped forward. "Y'all are getting the hang of it. How's it feel?"

The group lowered their swords and broke formation, laughing and patting each other on the back. Roxy answered with a proud smile, "Thanks, Etain. It's getting easier. How'd you learn to do that?"

She shrugged a shoulder. "I've done some reading and a lot of lurking in corners."

The redhead joined the two. "The way you explain it makes more sense. I'm glad Roxy and Tristan made me come."

"Thanks, Isobel."

G cleared his throat, turning the group his way. Most everyone returned to formation except Etain, who not having been subjected to his form of training, stood apart and stared at his approach. "What's this?"

A few eyes turned to Etain, but it was Isobel who bowed her head and spoke, "Good morning, Master. We've been practicing our lessons."

Etain gave the girl a side-eyed glance.

G lifted his chin at Isobel in the first instance. "Lessons?" His gaze slid to the silver-haired girl. "I don't recall any lunges in your training."

Etain matched his stance. "They can't just stand still and poke."

At G's flared nostrils, Sid came forward. "Let's get moving. I'm sure you all have somewhere else to be."

Angel held the door as the group shuffled from the room.

Once it was the four of them, G glared at Etain. "Most of these newbs have never held a sword much less *poked* with one. They've not had the same advantages as—" He sucked in a breath, his stern gaze going to Angel, who shrugged, moved to Sid and landed on the obstinate girl. "Why am I explaining myself to you? Get your ass downstairs, eat breakfast, and meet me in the small training room. Just you. We're going to find out what you're truly made of." He walked past her toward the door but stopped at her pronounced huff.

Etain narrowed her eyes, her grip so tight on her sword her knuckles turned white. She grabbed her pack and shoved her sword into the sheath. "Maybe if you hadn't *abandoned* me, I wouldn't have read the books in your tiny ass library or begun to wonder how the hell some of the moves detailed in those books actually *work*. Don't blame me if the others were curious. Those *newbs* as you call them are ready. Stop boring them with your drawn out, antiquated ways of training."

"When I want your help with training—or anything—not that I ever will since I've been doing this for years and years without your assistance—you'll be the first to know."

The three stood silent, listening to the click of his boots as he stalked down the hallway and descended the stairs. In a concerted release of breath, Angel closed the door. "Well. I'd say he got more than he bargained for."

Sid raised his brows, shoving his hands into his pockets. "Can't say as I recall anyone having the cojones to stand up to the man or tell him his training is shit."

Etain slung her pack onto her shoulder. "He was rude and offensive and from what I've heard, condescending. These people didn't choose this life and deserve to be treated with respect."

Sid leaned back against the wall. "He can be all those things. Believe me, we've seen worse. But don't think for a minute that he doesn't respect them or you. Me and Angel have seen plenty come and go—live and die." He pulled his hands from his pockets and pushed from the wall. "And for all we've seen, G's seen lots more—more death than life—and is determined to turn the odds more toward life, so excuse him if he moves at a slower pace. It's his way of making damn sure they're prepared for whatever this world throws at them."

Angel waved her hand. "Come on, then. It looks like you've been busy what with the destruction of your room and this one too. Did the library fare any better?"

Etain glanced at the shattered mirror. "I'd run out of steam by the time I got there."

"Good. I like visiting it from time to time." Angel followed her out of the room.

Sid came after them. "Smells like ya found the showers, too. Much appreciated. Are they still standing?"

The corner of her mouth lifted in a cheeky grin. "They're good."

"Let's get some breakfast. Between fixing mirrors, doors, and my other chores, I'm gonna have a pretty full day."

Her grin faded into a guilty pout. "Sorry, Sid. I didn't think about the fixing side of it."

"I don't imagine you did. I'll get Assassin X and Lord Darkness to help. You'll meet them later." He chuckled, back to his jovial self. "Me and Angel call it the G force. He has that effect on most people but once you get under his skin, he isn't so bad."

Etain shivered and rolled her eyes. "No thanks. I've seen enough."

Sid followed the two down the stairs. "Hell, girl. You ain't seen nothing yet."

⁂

While Sid and Angel filled their plates, Etain went to the long table where her fellow newbies sat.

"Hey, Etain." One particularly handsome dark-haired young man scooted down the bench offering her a seat. "You eating with us this morning?"

She appreciated the mischievous sparkle in his deep brown eyes. "Turlough, what're you doing sitting at the head of the table? I thought your place was at the end."

His white-toothed grin spread from ear to ear. "Ah, my fair lady, Etain. I'm afraid you've gotten turned around. This *is* the end of the table." He pointed toward the redhead dressed in a green jumpsuit at the opposite end. "You see? Wherever the lady Isobel sits is the head of the table even if she sits in the middle." He and the others around him laughed.

Isobel turned upon hearing the laughter, shot Turlough a searing golden-eyed glare, and rose, coming toward Etain. "Are you okay? I hope G didn't tear into you too bad."

Etain shrugged. "Just a little banter and repartee. I wish you could've been there."

Isobel trickled her fingers along the length of Etain's hair as though admiring the silver strands. "Don't let him get to you. He's a bit gruff but our wellbeing is his top priority. Will you be joining us today?"

"I've been ordered to the small training room, wherever that is."

Conversation at the table ceased and all eyes turned to her, some with their food suspended in mid-air, mouths hanging open. Isobel blinked several times, speechless. Etain eyed everyone, wondering *what the hell?* "Am I in trouble?"

Turlough lowered his fork and for once lost his glowing smile. "Hard to tell. Whose orders?"

In response to the serious faces around her, an impish sense of bravado took over. She responded in a heavy Southern accent, batting her eyelashes, and fanning her face with her hand. "Why, it was *Master* G himself. He was *most* insistent."

Varying degrees of widened eyes and cringes of horror flew around the table.

Etain bit her bottom lip and ran a hand through her hair. "It's bad, isn't it?"

Isobel sprung back to life, patting her on the shoulder. "It'll be fine. You'll be fine. I'm sure. He probably wants to know how you managed to get this lot together and in tune with one another."

Turlough raised a brow. "Yeah, make sure your sword isn't far away. His little chats can be brutal."

"Noted. Okay, well, y'all have a better day than me. Wish me luck."

Isobel gave her a heartfelt hug and whispered into her ear, "Thank you for your help. You got this."

Turlough bit into a piece of bacon and smiled. "He's the one who'll need the luck."

Etain almost laughed but caught herself. "Thanks, bud. Y'all wanna catch up tonight? Well, if I'm still alive?"

Her light-heartedness lifted the gloomy spell. The smiles returned as they resumed stuffing their faces, filling the room with their chatter.

Turlough scooted off his bench. "Etain. Just a sec." He linked an arm with hers and walked with her. "Thanks for the books," he whispered.

She stopped short. "Look, if this is one of your smartass—"

"*No.* No." He gave her a nervous smile, darting his eyes left and right before leaning toward her. "You were right. I was doing it *all* wrong. I've only tried a couple so far, but wow, yeah," he raised his hands to his temples, splaying his fingers out like an explosion, "mind blown. And the small book? Fuck me." He rolled his eyes back, smiling like a lunatic. "A whole new world."

She never expected he would read either book, much less put them to use. "I-I'm glad you enjoyed them."

He raised a brow over narrowed eyes. "Wanna join me in the library later? Hmm?"

*What have I done?* She gave him a halfhearted smile. "Oh, well, thanks, Turlough. How thoughtful. But I don't know how long I'll be with Master G."

"*Master* G? Yeah. Okay. Maybe some other time? I'll see you later." He returned to the others.

She crossed the room and joined Angel and Sid, who were well into their breakfasts.

"Everything all right?" Angel pushed a plate her way. "I gotcha a little something but get more if it's not enough."

Her stomach rolled. "I'd rather not eat at all."

"You gotta keep your energy up," Sid said, gnawing on his toast. "Meeting G on an empty stomach isn't the thing to do."

"Well, maybe it *would* be better to throw up my *breakfast* instead of my guts."

Sid choked on his food and coughed. Angel patted him on the back. "Heavens, Etain. The things that come out of your mouth. Are you okay, Sid? Here," she shoved a glass of water at him, "drink this."

Once his coughing subsided, he sipped at the water and laughed. "You be you. He loves to intimidate people. Don't let him get to you. It's time he got some push back from someone else besides my Angel."

His lady smiled and kissed him on the cheek. "He loves it." She turned to Etain. "Just stand your ground. And show him what you got."

Etain picked at her food. "Like what?"

Angel glanced at Sid, who sucked in a breath, raised his brows, and jumped into the pot. "The blue light thingy you do. That's what he's waiting for."

Etain pushed the plate away and slumped back in her chair. "I can't."

Angel set her elbows on the table and interlaced her fingers. "Why not?"

"I told you before." She lowered her voice. "Because of Jacob. I'm not taking another chance of hurting anyone."

"But he's fine."

"Yes, but only because he's a fire Alamir. What if it'd been Vivian or Vix? Would they have been so lucky?"

Sid leaned forward. "If you don't show him, he can't teach you how to control it."

Etain whispered in a harsh voice, "I can't just turn it on and off when I like."

Angel propped her chin on her interlaced fingers. "Oh, I think you can."

"What?"

"When G came at you the first night. It wasn't much different from when those young ones circled you in St. Clears. They had you cornered much like G did but with him, there was no flash of light. You took the hit and didn't bother to retaliate." She laid a hand over Etain's. "You held back. You *controlled* it." She squeezed her hand. "Show it to him. He'll teach you how to master it."

Etain held her gaze, fighting the burn in her eyes. "I have to be really, *really* upset for it to surface."

Sid snorted a laugh making others turn. "Don't you worry about that."

# MASTER G

Etain stepped into the room and quietly closed the heavy metal door, her gaze moving around the space as she set her pack on the floor. Daylight poured through rectangular windows along the top of the back wall. Their brightness along with the rounded lights in the ceiling and a mirrored wall kept the black room from closing in on her. Two chairs positioned in the center faced one another.

She opened the door hoping to catch Angel when a deep voice spoke, "You're in the right place."

G stood between the chairs dressed in jeans and untucked button-down shirt with the sleeves rolled up. What she interpreted as tribal tattoos covered his hands and traveled along his forearms. She met his gaze. "What is this?"

"Close the door and join me." He spread his arms over the chairs. "Let's chat."

Her eyes darted around the room as the door clicked closed. "About what?"

He clasped his hands in front of him. "Tell me about yourself."

The expression on his face and relaxed stance told her nothing but the hairs on the back of her neck spoke volumes. She shifted on her feet. "Why?"

His half ass smile leaned more toward a smirk. "Better the devil you know."

She laughed at his honesty and rolled her eyes. "Yeah. I get it." She grabbed her pack and ambled across the wooden floor toward the chairs. "I was expecting something like—"

A sandy brow rose. "Your first day here?"

The pack landed beside the first chair she came to, but instead of sitting, she faced the sandy-haired tough guy, trying to take in his measure. Well over six feet tall, clean shaven, broad shoulders, arms dusted with the same sandy hair, muscular everything, and hands the size of her head. But his features were refined. A not too long, narrow nose over nice lips and eyes the colors of the sea changing from green to blue and in between.

She started with a hand on her chest but soon reverted to expressive hand movements as she spoke. "I don't understand why everyone has to prove themselves at my expense. I don't want what they have. I'm not looking to take someone's place. I'm just another person who got caught up in something I didn't believe existed. I still wake up hoping it's nothing but a bad dream and mom or dad or even my brother will come into my room and drag me out for a family thing."

G eyed her from head to toe. "Aren't you a little old for the mommy-daddy attachment?"

She lowered her head but glanced up at him with hooded eyes. "No."

He scowled as he pulled back, placing his fingers over his mouth and staring at her. "No? Most girls your age want to be free and on their own."

"Most girls my age like to act that way but when it comes down to it, they're full of shit. I'm smart enough to know we aren't ready for it."

G rubbed his chin. "Not ready for what?"

Etain lifted her head and crossed her arms over her chest. "To be alone. Without a clue of what to do or how to do it, whatever *it* is, or who to trust. Not enough life experience."

He chuckled. "Sounds like a pampered princess syndrome."

She hissed through bared teeth and dropped her arms, balling her hands into fists at her sides. "Do *not* make fun of me or my family. Every girl should be a pampered princess at least once in her fucking life before the shitty ass world pukes its garbage all over her. And this world is about as shitty as it gets."

G raised his hands as though shielding himself. "Etain. I'm sorry. I didn't bring you here to be insulted. I was only teasing."

She narrowed her eyes. "Have you seen what teasing does to hair? Don't do it with someone you don't know. You'll end up with a nasty rat nest."

His lips thinned as he lowered his hands. "Big talk from a—"

She lunged at him. "A little girl? Yeah. A little girl in a big man's world. We'll see how big it is once I'm done with it." Her body shook fighting to quell her anger, flexing and squeezing her hands into balls several times. *God, I need to scream!* So she did. Loud, intense, and long until she collapsed to her knees.

G bore the brunt of her rage as though a lighthouse in a violent storm. Once she quieted, he crouched in front of her, his voice soft. "Etain. This hasn't gone as I intended. I can see your family is important to you. Tell me your story. I can't fix what's happened, but I can help you become the warrior you're so desperate to become."

She swiped at her nose and pushed her hair from her face. "It's not *wanting* to be a warrior. It's a requirement. It's what I must do. I must *be*. So I can defend those who can't fight. Protect them from the scum who prey on others."

"Shit." G moved into the other chair, resting his elbows on his knees. "Etain. How old are you?"

She ran a hand through her hair and blurted without thinking, "Fourteen." After sucking in a breath, she cursed, "Damn."

G leaned back, propped his chin on his hand, and stared at her. "Damn?"

Her head in her hands, she forced herself to look at him. "I swore I wouldn't say it again."

"That you're fourteen?"

"No one believes me because of this." She slapped her chest. "This body is my 'gift' from the Alamir. And my boots."

His gaze went to her leather knee-high, lace up boots, with soles so serious they would make a military man salivate. "Steel toed?"

"Yeah."

He wiped a hand over his face. "Okay. Well, it gives me another perspective."

Etain pulled herself up and into the other chair. Although he appeared to be deep in thought, she asked, "Do you still want to talk?"

His gaze met hers as though he'd forgotten she was there. "You're damn right I want to talk. Start wherever you're most comfortable."

She lifted her chin. "I don't need you or anyone else feeling sorry for me."

He gritted his teeth for a moment. "Is pity what're you're expecting?"

"Fuck this." She gripped the arms of her chair.

"Stop." G leaned forward. "Look at what you've achieved since your arrival." He held up a finger. "Of your own volition, might I add. Neither of us has time for pity, so trust me with your story. What is said in this room today will *not* be shared unless you decide to tell someone else. The more I know, the easier it will be to devise a lesson plan to suit you, and in the long run, benefit others."

"Trust?" Etain curled her feet under her and picked at the laces of a boot. "I don't trust anyone...or myself."

G clapped his hands together and stood. "Then we'll start there."

A corner of her lip curled up. "Huh?"

"Trust."

She uncurled her legs, setting her feet on the floor. "How?"

"Shall we start with this?" He smiled as he called out, "Sid!"

Etain stared at G until she noticed a door open in one of the black walls. Sid stepped in followed by another person. In a quandary over what was occurring, she glanced at G again and came to her feet as the men neared. Tears formed as they approached. "Jacob?"

The man looked as though he would cry, too, but managed to hold back the tears. and welcomed her into his embrace.

"Etain," Jacob whispered in his gruff voice. "It's good to see you."

She downright cried in his arms. "I thought I'd— Holy shit, I thought you were—"

"You packed a wallop, I can't lie." He let her go and winked. "Took me a couple of days, but I'm fine now."

After a swipe at her tears, she eyed him from head to toe. "I'm so sorry. I didn't—"

Jacob pulled a handkerchief from his back pocket and handed it to her. "It's fresh. Not been used. You saved my life is what you did. If you hadn't hit that ugly thing, I *would* be dead."

"Thank you." A pout on her lips, she dabbed at her cheeks and nose. "Are you sure?"

"You did the right thing. I'm glad you made it out of there. I'll sleep easier knowing you're in a good place."

*That's yet to be determined.* She wrapped her arms around herself. "How's Vivian? Is Vix okay? What about the others?"

Jacob nodded and smiled. "All good. No casualties. On our side." He winked again. "Once they realized you were gone, they cleared out."

She ran a hand through her hair. "Oh. Well, as long as everyone's safe."

"I gotta admit, we've been sick with worry wondering what happened to you. We breathed easier when Sid confirmed they'd found you and got you to G."

Her eyes widened as she raised both brows and slipped her hands into her pockets, handkerchief included. "Yeah. Angel told me you were okay, but I gotta admit, I didn't believe her."

G slapped him on the back. "Thank you for coming, Jacob. I'm sure you'd like to catch up with Sid and Angel."

Etain stepped forward. "But I want to talk to him."

G turned to her. "You will. Later."

"Don't worry, Etain," Jacob assured her with a warm smile. "I'm not going anywhere until we talk. Vivian would kill me if I didn't come back with every detail of what's happened since you left us." He laughed reciprocating a powerful slap on G's back. "Don't take it too far, mister, or you'll answer to me."

After Jacob and Etain shared another hug, he and Sid exited through the same door they'd entered earlier. She stared at G, who having waited until they were gone, turned to Etain. He appeared caught off guard by her intense stare.

"Why'd you bring him here?"

He lifted his chin and clasped his hands behind his back. "Trust."

It sounded like bullshit and smelled of it. But this place was a lot better than being alone and living rough. "Trust?"

"It's a long shot, but maybe if you learn to trust me, you'll let me help you to trust yourself."

She cocked her head to the side and slid her hands into her back pockets. "So, because you brought Jacob here, I'm supposed to trust you?"

"Jacob is confirmation that what comes from the mouths of my Darth people, including myself, is truth." Obviously chuffed with himself, he smiled and returned to his seat. "And I, in return, *did* leave you with my newbies."

"Trust *you*?" She sucked her teeth and crossed her arms again, pacing. "After the insane mind fuck you put me through my first night here? Or the fact I was left on my own for *weeks*?"

He chuckled, watching her walk back and forth. "A test. You weren't in any danger."

She stood still. "I wasn't *afraid*. I had no concern for *my* safety. Would you like to know what I think?"

He lifted a brow.

Her arms fell to her sides. "I think you forgot about me. Or. You're at a loss about what to do with me." She leaned toward him over the back of her chair, gripping each of its arms. "I was *angry*."

G propped his elbows on the arms of his chair and steepled his fingers. "So you smashed a few mirrors and destroyed some toilets. It kept you occupied and out of trouble."

The words spilled distinctly from her snarling frown of a mouth, her gaze piercing into his. "Did you at any time consider the safety of anyone else in this mausoleum? Imagine if someone had pierced through your façade. Or if I had ripped it apart and continued down the stairs, going room by room, terrorizing, destroying, possibly hurting innocent people."

Her accusation wiped the smile from his face. "I would have stepped in and stopped you."

She slid over the back of the chair and crouched in the seat. "Even if you *had* been here, I'm sure you'd *wanted* to. But." She raised a brow. "*Could* you? You don't have a fucking clue what I can do. I know you've heard stories, but *you* haven't *seen* it. You haven't *experienced* it."

One booted foot stomped on the floor followed by the other, her steeled gaze holding his as she grabbed her pack. "The next time you wanna bait me with your bullshit games, I suggest you have a chat with Jacob."

She stalked from the room, waited until the door clicked closed, and kicked it with all her might, only because she couldn't slam it. "Fuck you and this place."

When she turned, several others in the hallway stared at her and the large dent in the door. She shifted her pack on her shoulder. "There was a bug."

---

G remained in his seat for several minutes, contemplating what had happened. From the information gathered from Vivian, Jacob, Sid, and Angel, she wasn't a troublemaker or fabricator of stories. She didn't seek attention from others. She was a kid trying to survive in an adult world. *A magical one at that.*

He rubbed his forehead at the memory of her first night there and his ingenious plan to force her to reveal her power. *What an anime goon you've become G. Believing your own bullshit so much you ignore the signs of a soul in distress.*

Her conviction to protect others made sense now. No one had protected her. Not until she met Vivian and Jacob. Her time with them was so short, none of them believed a bond had formed. Evidently, it had. Seeing Jacob fall from her attack on the goblin explained why she was reluctant to release it again.

"Clusterfuck." He swiped a hand over his face. "A goddamned clusterfuck."

The approach of footsteps made him look up. Instead of Sid, it was another member of the Darth clan, Azrael, tall, long dark hair, and leathered wings to match. "Not what you were expecting."

"Hell no." G pushed out of the chair. "She is an enigma. One minute she's a kid and has me thinking she needs my help. In the next, she's an old hag spouting wisdom she shouldn't possess."

Azrael covered his mouth as he laughed. "Sorry, G. I can't recall the last time I saw you so perplexed."

G growled. "You can't recall because it's never happened." Then he laughed. "This one's going to challenge us all, Az. Tell the others to be prepared. And get these chairs the hell out of here. Starting tomorrow, it's full-on."

"I'll get Lord Darkness to stock up on the medicals and put the rest of the clan on alert."

Etain stepped onto what she thought was her floor. Groups of people loitered in the hallway chatting while others moved furniture in and out of rooms. She stepped back into the stairwell and counted the floors. "It's definitely the second floor."

When she returned to the chaos, Isobel linked an arm with hers. "Etain. There you are. Come see what we've done with your room. You're going to love it."

Etain frowned, eyeing the hustle bustle as they strolled the hallway. "What've you done to my room? Why're all these people on my floor?" She pulled Isobel out of the way of an oncoming dresser. "Watch it, man!"

"Man? Who says that anymore?" The redhead giggled. "It's not *your* floor. It's just *a* floor."

"It was *my* floor until all of you showed up."

Isobel snuggled up to her and laid her head on her shoulder as they continued down the hall. "You can't be all by yourself. We must stick together."

"Why?" Etain rolled her eyes, wishing the girl and everyone else would fuck off. "What's wrong with *your* floor and their floors?"

"Don't be a grump just because G is mean." Isobel let go and skipped ahead opening the door to Etain's room. "Tristan even fixed the door. Voilà! Isn't it cozy?"

Etain groaned as she entered her room, certain if it was designed by Isobel, it would be a disaster. To her surprise, it wasn't so bad. Sheer violet panels softened the light coming through the window and complemented the soft, furry duvet in the same violet on the bed. A deep red scarf thrown over the lamp complimented a rich fabric of mixed colors draped on the chair—violet, deep red, gold, bronze—so many varying shades she couldn't decipher them all.

Isobel smiled at her with eyes wide. "Do you like it?"

Etain set her pack on the floor next to the bed as she surveyed the room. "It's perfect. I love violet. How'd you—"

She raised her hands in a shrug. "It's what I do. I can't explain it. I just...know."

Etain caressed the furry duvet and sat on the bed. "Oh my god."

"I know, right? Pure decadence." Isobel moved closer and sat on the other side of the bed, touching the soft fur. "It's fake but it feels real."

"Where'd you find it?"

"In one of these rooms. It doesn't look like anyone's been up here ever. Not until you came. So everyone's picking and choosing, trading and sharing, making these rooms ours. It's much nicer than where we were."

Etain shifted onto the bed and leaned against the headboard. "You saw how drab this room was until you got hold of it. I tried getting into the other rooms, but the doors were locked."

Isobel stretched across the bed on her belly and propped her head on her hands, a dreamy cast in her gold eyes. "They were open when we invaded."

Etain moved away from the headboard, coming face to face with the girl, and grinned. "Well, I guess we're gonna get real chummy being on the same floor."

It was meant as a joke but the dreaminess in Isobel's eyes shifted into what Etain could only describe as hope. A soft breath escaped from the girl's parted lips. Etain met her intense golden gaze with one of curiosity, wondering at the flutter in her chest, and the sudden awkwardness between them.

Isobel's gaze dipped to Etain's lips, her voice a breathy whisper. "Make sure to lock your door." Her eyes came back to hers. "Unless you *want* company during the night. Or any time, really. Not everyone understands boundaries." As if asking for permission, her lips, soft and uncertain, pressed against Etain's.

She reveled in the whisper of a shared warmth, closed her eyes and let her heart answer, forgetting the world around them. No music, no fireworks. For Etain, it was enough to be seen by another person and accepted.

When they parted, Etain swallowed, biting the inside of her bottom lip, wanting to speak but didn't know what to say. Isobel didn't seem to mind the silence. It allowed them both a moment of needed solitude to adjust to an unexpected level of their friendship.

Etain twisted off the bed. "Shall we join the others and make their rooms as cozy as mine?"

Isobel considered her for a moment longer and rolled off the bed. "We have class. Want to come with?"

"Hmph. Am I allowed?"

Isobel grabbed her hand and pulled her to the door. "Let's see what happens."

# GOBLINS

"**S**omeday, you might face—" Azrael rested a hand on his chest and bowed his head. "No. I must correct myself. Apologies, young Alamir. Someday, you *will* face a life-or death situation where it's either you or your opponent."

A student Etain didn't recognize commented, "But we'll be with our clan. We'll fight together to defeat our enemy."

Azrael whirled toward the voice. "Will you? Do you know anything about *being* in a clan?"

The student shrugged. "We've all talked about it."

Their instructor nodded. "Please share the conversation with the class."

The young man frowned and lowered his eyes. "We were talking about which clan we want to join when we leave here."

Azrael's eyes deepened to black. "Were you? And which clan have you decided on, Janiken?"

His blue-eyed gaze met his instructor's, filled with conviction. "*.com*. They're strong fighters and have each other's backs."

"Good luck with that, Jani," Turlough sniggered. "I'm set on FWH. Fight with Honor."

Roxy laughed. "Stop it. They're so big, you'd get lost in the crowd."

A grin lit his face. "Yeah, the female part." Everyone laughed as he wiggled his brows.

"LOKI sounds like a good clan," Tristan said. "They're strong fighters, too."

Janiken shook his head. "If you're looking to stab someone in the back."

Etain's training partner, Tristan, a handsome, shaggy headed blond with eyes as blue as the sea, sucked in an offended breath. Although she didn't quite understand the animosity between the two, she asked, "Why do you say that? Surely, if they're Alamir, they're an honorable clan."

"Ha! A clan of mercenaries led by a ruthless merc. If you see one coming, you better run the other way."

Tristan's hands balled into fists. "Lord Darknight is an honorable chieftain and expects nothing but the best from his clan."

Janiken laughed. "Sure, Tristan. Tell that to the next clan LOKI bashes. When they join the fight, they take no prisoners."

Etain furrowed her brows. "Can that be true?" She turned round until she found their instructor. "Milord, do they kill other Alamir?"

Azrael stopped his slow pace around the teams, his leather wings looming over his shoulders. "LOKI *is* a formidable clan."

"How can the Ambassadors condone such behavior in the Alamir? This Lord Darknight should be exiled and his clan disbanded."

With a thoughtful rise of his brows, Azrael continued his slow pace around the students. "From the mouths of babes."

Etain pressed her lips together, raking her tongue through her teeth, and chewing the inside of her mouth. Tristan leaned toward her and whispered, "Just let it go."

Her back straight, she glared at the instructor with hooded eyes. "I am not here to kill other Alamir."

Tristan shook his head. "It's your funeral."

Azrael expressed a thoughtful smirk, snapping his black leather wings out and tucking them close to his body. "Aside from Janiken's colorful conjecture, what if it *is* another Alamir?"

Her head swiveled, waiting for someone to state the obvious. When nothing came, she blurted, "We have the Mobius Arena."

Several pairs of eyebrows rose, including Azrael's. "You are familiar with the arena?"

Others around her exchanged nervous glances, asking what it was. Tristan pressed his lips together in a show of sympathy.

She shot a conspiratorial smile his way and shrugged. "Only through stories."

Azrael clasped his hands behind his back as he walked toward her. "Did these stories mention what is said about the arena?"

She cleared her throat and swallowed. "Uh, two walk in," her gaze roamed over those closest to her, "b-but might not walk out."

Tristan stared at her and mouthed, *how do you know?*

She blinked in return.

"Correct!" Azrael exclaimed, releasing his hands and pointing a finger in the air much like her teachers back home would do. "Please bear with me, my young Alamir."

He stood next to Etain and Tristan. "Let's say another Alamir is determined to take your life for whatever reason. Do you believe their next thought will be of the Mobius Arena?" He paused for a moment, eyeing his students. "And not only will they be able to put aside their ire and passion until a later time, but also be willing to set a date for your demise?"

It sounded ridiculous hearing it said aloud. Her hand twitched at her side, wanting to shove it through her hair. "Alamir are supposed to work together against the *Bok*, not each other."

"In theory. Yes." His smile made her stomach turn. "Tell me, Etain. How do you determine who is Alamir and who is *Bok*?"

All eyes were on her. She chewed her bottom lip while her mind raced for an answer. No one had made the distinction between the two, and frankly, she hadn't thought about it. *Did they wear a uniform? Were they as ugly as the goblins?*

Azrael turned his attention to the class. "Anyone? Who can tell us the difference in appearance between the *Bok* and Alamir?"

Then she remembered. "Brown uniforms. The *Bok* wore brown military style uniforms."

A shiver ran through the instructor's leathered wings and a grimace flashed across his face. In the next instant, he stroked his chin, his face returning to its neutral expression. It made her wonder at his experiences with the *Bok*.

"Another story?"

*Shit!* This was to be a new start. A new life. No mention of the goblins or *Bok* who'd come to take her because of... Because she was... *What?* Because of her *blue light thingy* as Sid called it?

Azrael stood in front of her, jarring her from her thoughts. "Good. You're back with us. Please share how you know the *Bok* wear brown uniforms."

Her heart hammered, holding his piercing blue gaze. *Don't back down. Just give 'em the highlights.* Sweat beaded on her brow and in her pits. She cleared her throat again and switched her sword to the other hand wiping the sweat from her palm onto her jeans.

"Well, there was a fight." Her gaze swept over the others in the room. Noting their interest, she continued, "In a small town south of here. It involved men in brown uniforms."

A deep crease showed between Azrael's dark brows. "Did you base your assumption on the color of their uniforms? We have several clans who wear brown."

"No. I based it on the fact they fought beside goblins."

A unified gasp passed through the others. The sudden paleness of Azrael's face assured her she'd made an impression.

"Goblins? A-Are you certain?"

"About ten feet tall, as ugly as you can imagine, and green." She doubted it was actually ten feet. Probably more like eight or nine. *Who has time to measure when you're fighting for your life?*

Mouths dropped open, eyes filled with horror, and someone let out a small scream.

Apparently, it was enough. "Alamir, you are dismissed."

Although their instructor left the training room, the other students grouped around Etain, firing questions at her one after another.

"Did you really fight goblins?"

"I did."

"What's a goblin?"

"Like I said, big ugly green creatures."

"Are they really green?"

Etain rolled her eyes and glared.

"How'd you get away?"

"I ran like hell."

"Why were the *Bok* there?"

"Don't know. They just showed up."

She did her best to answer every question without admitting the real why she and the *Bok* were in the same place at the same time. Jacob was not mentioned, and neither was her special power.

Later in the day, after the group settled into their new rooms, Etain broke away and headed downstairs hoping to find Jacob. She thought herself most fortunate when she met him with Sid and Angel in the foyer at the main doors.

"Jacob. You *are* here." She wanted to hug him but held back. "Hey, Angel, Sid. What've y'all been up to?"

Jacob laughed. "Looking for you."

"What?" *Did I just waste time I could've been spending with him or—*

"Stop your fretting, *merch*." Jacob chuckled. "We figured you had your hands full after your interview with G and only just decided to come to you."

"How'd it go?" Angel asked. Sid leaned forward, a hint of a smile on his lips.

Etain shrugged. "He pissed me off. Of course. But he didn't get what he expected."

Angel grabbed Sid's hand. "Did you show him your light?"

She ran a hand through her hair. "He doesn't deserve to see it."

Jacob draped an arm over her shoulders. "Let's not spend our time talking about him. Is there somewhere we can sit and chat about where you've been and what you've done? I have a woman waiting back home who's anxious for news."

"Let's go to our apartments," Angel offered. "We can chat all we want and not be interrupted."

"Sounds good to me," Etain said, happy to get away from the craziness of the place. "Can we eat in your apartment, or do we have to go to the commissary?"

Angel caught Jacob's eye. "Do you remember how to get back?"

"Aye. What do you have in mind?"

She handed a key to the big man. "You and Etain go ahead." She winked as she pulled Sid in the opposite direction. "We'll meet you there."

He glanced at Etain with a furrowed brow. "What was that about?"

"I'm pretty sure Angel's gone to chat with the chef."

A huge smile spread across his face. "Well, sounds a plan. Shall we walk on?" She linked her arm with his as they strolled down the hallway. "So how was it after you left us?"

"Horrible. I ended up in some crappy little town full of angry Alamir."

He patted her hand wrapped around his arm. "Seems like many a chip was laid on many a shoulder. I've seen it meself. I'm sorry you had to see it too."

Jacob was the calming influence she didn't realize she needed. Her heartbeat slowed and the tension faded as they walked through the hallways. Coming to a door similar to her own, Jacob pulled the key from his pocket and opened into a warm and comfy abode decorated in the colors of autumn.

She smiled as she entered. "It almost feels like home."

"Aye. I thought the same thing when I first saw it. Angel is a special lady." He closed the door and followed her to the double sofas positioned in front of an oversized fireplace. "Would you like a brew, milady?"

She shook her head as she curled up on a sofa. "I could kill for a sweet tea, but it'd be a senseless murder."

"Sweet tea?" Jacob held up a finger. "Give me a minute."

She called after him. "I'm not talking about a cup of tea with sugar. It's a drink we had back home." If he came back with a cup of sweetened tea, she'd happily drink it. As long as she could stay in this place with these people who didn't want anything from her or expect her to be something she wasn't. No blue light, no shining warrior, and no giving what she didn't have to give.

Jacob walked into the room with a glass in each hand—one filled with an amber brew topped by an impressive head and the other strongly resembling... She uncurled her legs with eyes wide. "Is it really?"

He handed it to her with a soft smile. "Angel tried to get me to drink it earlier but being the Welsh lad I am, it isn't me cup of tea."

Etain laughed, accepting the glass. "Master G should put Angel in charge. She'd get a lot more out of these people than he ever will."

Jacob sat on the sofa across from her and propped one leg over the other. "He's a different breed, for sure. But don't let his gruff exterior turn you off. He's done more good than not."

She sipped her tea and sighed, "Heavenly," setting it on the side table. "Sid kinda said the same thing. But you know what? I'm a different breed, too. He *wanted* me to come here. I was fine doing what I was doing."

He raised a heavy brow. "Getting damn near slaughtered by goblins?"

She pressed her lips together. "I meant before."

"*Merch*, I'm afraid you're not meant for a casual life amongst the Alamir." He held up a hand in anticipation of her rebuke. "Like it or not, you have a special gift and there'll be those who want to take it, own it, or control it. Lucky for you, we're here to support and teach you how to either avoid them or defend yourself. So does G."

She rolled her eyes. "All he wants is to *see* my power."

He enjoyed a swig of his brew and wiped the foam from his beard. "The man's gotta see what he has to work with first. Let down your guard and I promise he'll do the same."

"Hmph. If I let down my guard, he'll kick my ass."

Jacob laughed loud and long. "By the Gods, won't he just?"

Etain rolled her eyes again but laughed with him and picked up her tea. "Okay. For you Jacob, I'll try harder."

"*Dyna fi ferch* (That's me girl)!"

Upon Angel and Sid's return with supper, the four worked together setting the table, laying out the food, and sharing stories well into the night.

Etain yawned and stretched. "I think it's time to head to my room. Tomorrow's my first real class and I want to be ready. Thank y'all for a great night." As she neared the door, Sid came from out of nowhere and blocked her way. "Sid?" A small laugh hummed behind her lips. "What're you doing?"

He clasped his hands in front of him and shrugged a shoulder. "Stay here tonight. We have plenty of room."

"Why? My room isn't far. It won't take—"

Angel came forward, smiling as though everything was fine, but Etain sensed the undercurrent of a different story. "It *is* late, hun. We'll make sure you're up in time and share breakfast with Jacob before he leaves."

The big man spoke from where he stood as though he were part of the conspiracy. "You can stay in my room. I don't mind sleeping out here."

*What are they up to?* She eyed Jacob for a moment and moved on to Angel, running her tongue over her teeth, and ended her scrutiny with Sid. "Why can't I go to my room?"

The three exchanged glances but it was Jacob who spoke. "Better we tell her."

Etain crossed her arms over her chest. "*What?*"

Jacob sighed. "I'm not here for you, *merch*."

A pang hit her in the heart. She tried to keep it from transferring to her face or voice and failed on both counts. "B-But Master G said—"

Jacob held his hands out with palms up, "I brought in a few rogue Alamir who've been making noises about turning *Bok*. He mentioned you were here and asked if I'd like to see you."

Cheeks on fire, her arms dropped to her sides. "So, it had nothing to do with trust."

Jacob frowned, a crease deepening between his brows.

"Great." She lowered her head, biting her bottom lip. "Good to know."

"Well, then," Angel rested a hand on Etain's shoulder, "let's get to—"

Etain nailed the woman with a glare, shrugging off her hand. "None of this explains why I can't go to my room. Unless it has to do with the rogue Alamir Jacob brought here." She zeroed in on him. "I thought this was a training site for newbies, not a rehab for the confused."

Jacob lowered his head and ran a hand over his head. "*Gan y saint.*"

Sid stepped away from the door. "New ones aren't the only ones who need help, Etain. Sometimes if we catch those teetering between good and evil soon enough, we can set 'em straight."

Etain frowned and nodded. "Fine. Great. I'm going to my room."

As she turned toward the door, Sid blocked her again. "No, you're not. You're staying here until morning."

She blinked. "Aren't they locked up somewhere? You think they'd be running around the complex?"

His face turned to stone. "We're not taking the chance, especially with you. The door is locked for the evening and not even you can get through it."

Etain clenched her jaws, her mouth dry. A cold sweat spread across her forehead and her heart beat in hyperdrive. "No." she whispered, glaring at the three simultaneously.

Angel reached for her.

"Don't' touch me," she growled and turned to Sid. "Open the door."

He straightened to his full height, arms loose at his sides. "Go to bed. We're not going anywhere—"

An image of blue fire manifested in her mind.

⁂

Jacob attributed a spark of light over Sid's head as his imagination or even the light messing with his eyes due to it having been a long day. When another one sparked above Angel, bursting into a barrage of blue stars and showering over her, he lunged from his spot, shielding her with his body.

She shrieked in surprise but held onto him. With a twist, the two collided into Sid, crushing him into the door.

Jacob pressed his hands to the wall and gritted his teeth against the sharp pin pricks assailing his broad shoulders and back. "*Gan y Duwiau! Sut ydyn ni'n gwneud iddi stopio?*"

"In English, man!" Sid muttered.

"Sorry." Jacob grimaced at the electrical onslaught. "How do we stop her?"

The smirk on Sid's lips didn't help. "I don't even know how we started it."

Angel ducked her head as sparks flashed above them. "She doesn't like having her back against a wall."

Sid's eyes bugged. "No one touched the girl."

"Metaphorically, hard head. She feels trapped."

Realization dawned in his eyes. "Ah. So she's having a temper tantrum, is she?"

The situation broken down into its purest form, Jacob guffawed, his entire body shaking from the effort. "Sid, *rydych chi'n wirioneddol ddwfn, fy ffrind.*"

"In English, ya crazy Welshman." But he and his wife couldn't help but laugh with the man.

Jacob wiped his forehead along the sleeve of his shirt. "You're a deeper man than I give you credit for."

"If it's a compliment, thank you." He narrowed his eyes. "If not, burn in hell. But we have bigger problems. She's gone."

Jacob realized the pin pricks had ceased and looked over one shoulder and the other. Sure enough, she wasn't there. "*Gan y saint*. We best go find her."

# BLUE STAR ENIGMA

Etain raised a hand to avoid stumbling into a concrete wall. Steady on her feet, she pushed the hair away from her face with the other and gazed at an unfamiliar landscape. "What the hell?"

A few steps away from the wall, she scrutinized the structure. "It's the same building but this isn't the same place." Gone were the pink and purple moors. No hills. No valleys. She found herself in a labyrinth of trees, young, old, tall, thick, thin, and short. The air smelled different. *Probably because of the trees?* Spicy, sweet mixed with damp. She shivered from the coolness rising from the forest floor.

"Did I do this?" She walked to the end of wall and peered around the corner. More trees. "Or is it another test from Master G?"

She circled around the entire structure. There were no windows, no doors, no entrance or exit of any sort. She tried slapping the walls, but they sounded as solid as they looked.

"Great." She leaned back and was thankful for the warmth coming from the wall. "Do I stand here and wait, hoping someone will notice I'm gone?"

Chewing her bottom lip, her thoughts returned to what happened in Sid and Angel's apartment. "There were sparks. Blue sparks. Above Sid's head." She paced in one direction, working it out. "And Angel's. Holy crap, Etain. You lost control. Idiot!"

After a face palm to the forehead, she turned in the other direction. "Man, maybe they aren't interested in finding me."

A sudden realization made her stop. "They have no idea where I am. Shit."

She took in the measure of the concrete structure, judging its height, and glanced at the trees. *I can't see anything down here. But maybe if I…*

It took a few precious minutes to circle around the building again and reconfirm there was no way in or out, or up. Surrounded by so many trees, she chose the closest one and made a run at it, scrambling up its trunk almost within reach of the lowest branch. It wasn't big enough to carry her weight, but it could possibly give her a boost toward the larger branches above. The rubber soles of her boots gripped the bark, taking her within millimeters of touching the branch, but made it difficult to get her feet in the right position. "Damn!" She pushed away and landed on the ground with a grunt.

She tried again. This time, the small branch grazed her fingertips. With gritted teeth, she pushed with her legs and stretched her body to its full height, her mind willing her arm to stretch even further. Blowing out a breath, she made a grab for the damn thing. A rush of satisfaction made her smile. In the next moment, the branch snapped. She fell backward and landed on the ground with a resounding 'oof!'

Sucking in a few breaths, she sat up, glaring at the tree. "You'd think I'd have the hang of this by now." She removed her boots, stuffed her socks inside, and tied the laces together, draping them over her shoulders and made another run. Sheer determination and bare feet helped her climb to one branch and another.

The forest, suddenly alive with sounds, seemed to be laughing at her, daring her to break through the leafy canopy, slapping her cheeks until they burned, pulling at her hair, and scratching at every exposed bit of skin. The young warrior persevered until she reached a branch large enough to support her weight.

The branch gripped firmly in her hands, she peered through the leafy canopy and was rewarded with a sight of the building's rooftop. "Grass? Master G's an eco-warrior?"

Laughing at her wit, she latched an arm over the branch, wincing at the rough bark and tiny shoots scratching the soft skin underneath, while she worked the boots from around her neck and tossed them onto the roof. *Please don't disappear.*

A blustery wind joined the party adding to her precarious situation of dangling high above the forest floor. She held onto the swaying branch with both hands and inched along its length, doing her best to ignore the cuts and scratches of the tree's last-ditch efforts to be rid of her. "Just a little farther and you'll be free of me forever."

Finally at the edge of the rooftop, she closed her eyes and sucked in a breath. "Make it count." She repositioned her hands on the branch, twisting her body toward the rooftop, and swung back and forth. Once she had momentum, she let go of the branch and sailed through the air, landing ungraciously on the roof.

Fortunately for her, the grass softened the fall. There would be bruising but better than hitting concrete. "Damn." She pushed to her feet and surveyed the area. Trees—as far as she could see. "How the heck did he get it in here?"

She grabbed her boots and sat, untying the laces from one another. With them strapped on again, she lay back, staring at the leafy sky above. "I wonder where we'll go next." She rested an arm across her forehead, blocking the light from her heavy eyes.

While Angel and Jacob searched floor by floor for the missing girl, Sid headed to G's suite to inform him of the situation. G opened the door, his expression as rough as his greeting. "What is it?"

"We have a situation."

"Have the rogues broken free?" He moved to close the door. "Get Jacob on it."

"Well, no. The rogues are safely locked away."

G raised a stern brow. "Then what the hell is it?"

Sid clasped his hands behind his back. "It's Etain."

G lowered his head and sighed. "What now?"

He refused to let the man's hard gaze intimidate him. The girl was in trouble. "She's disappeared."

"Sid." G leaned against the door. "How is this *my* problem?"

"It's not what you think."

"And what do I think?"

"She was with us and Jacob in our apartment. We had dinner and a nice visit until late. When it came time for bed, she insisted on returning to her room."

"Of course, you told her no."

Sid pressed his lips together and nodded. "Yes. We all did. Told her she could stay with us, and we'd go to breakfast together."

G sighed and yawned.

His blasé attitude rubbed Sid the wrong way. "You remember the thing you were hoping to see when we brought her here?"

The big man straightened. "What happened?"

Sid had his attention, but the man was distracted, scrutinizing Sid's head instead of meeting his gaze. "What're you looking at?"

G narrowed his eyes and leaned toward him. "When did you get a tattoo?"

He self-consciously touched his head. "Tattoo?"

G grabbed his arm and dragged him through the apartment to the bathroom, stood him in front of the mirror and pointed at the hairline on the left side of his forehead. "That."

Sid noticed the mark and leaned closer to the mirror. "It's just a bit of dirt, I'm sure." He tapped his finger on his tongue and rubbed at the blue star. When it didn't go away, he leaned closer to the mirror. "Oh. Well. I'll be damned."

G disappeared into the bedroom. "Get the rest of the clan up and searching. She's here somewhere. I'll start with the basement. Let's meet in the small training room in an hour."

"Yessir." Sid rubbed his forehead one last time. "I'll be damned." Without another word, he left G to dress and went in search of the blue star enigma.

⁓·❦❦·⁓

Things were different. The scent of the forest was heavy and more damp than before. A chill covered her skin. The ground beneath her back was cold and the quiet palpable. She lifted her arm from across her forehead, and even though dark surrounded her, noticed she was no longer amid the treetops.

"Where's the building?" She ran a shaky hand through her hair and a burn threatened in her eyes as she stood, checking each direction. "They left me." Coming full circle, twinkling lights caught her eye. "Okay. They left me. I have to get them to come back. So, do I find fresh Alamir or go for the rogue?"

At the edge of the forest, the path Etain followed fed into a wide well-worn road and rambled into the distance. The twinkling lights didn't seem to be much closer than when she first saw them, but it gave her a destination and hopefully, she'd find someone willing to help.

No one passed her along the way but there were scattered lights on either side set back from the road. She figured them to be outlying homes, which meant the town wasn't much further.

Around the next bend, the buildings appeared more prevalent yet still scattered. Those few doubled and tripled. The buildings were quaint, not one was over two stories, and appeared as old as the hills. Black wrought iron lamps alight with small blazing flames cast a cozy glow over the cobbled roads and faces of the shops. She hugged herself against the chill of the night.

Standing at a crossroads, she glanced right and left, shrugged, and stayed on the path into the middle of town. People hustled and bustled around her. Some shops were in the midst of turning off lights and locking doors.

She came to a lively establishment on her left and smiled. Through the window she watched families enjoying their suppers, jolly looking men standing at a bar laughing over a brew, while waitresses weaved their way through the groups delivering food or serving drinks. *Welcoming, well lit, and safe*. A guaranteed attraction to a newbie freshly landed in the Alamir world.

Music from across the road made her turn to what appeared to be its evil brother. *Dark, menacing, and secretive*. The windows were either blacked out or covered as no light escaped through them. Perfect for a rogue to find likeminded Alamir wanting to transition.

She ambled into the middle of the road, contemplating which one to enter. *Light and safe? Or dark and mysterious?* Just as she was coming to a decision, a man's light-hearted voice interrupted her thoughts.

"Decisions, decisions. Which path would the lady be taking?" A tall, light-haired young man dressed in black leather armor and cloak circled around her from behind. His Irish accent was lovely, but his smile didn't sit well with her. She'd seen enough arrogance to recognize it in this one. Despite her dodging his hand, his smile didn't waiver as he reached out and pulled a leaf from her hair. "I'm thinking you should be headed to a bath house instead of a pub. Had a rough day?"

She ran a hand through her hair and discovered a few more leaves. "I-I took a shortcut through the woods."

He narrowed an eye and leaned toward her. "What would a lovely like yerself be doing in the woods? And without a cloak, no less. Were ya having an evening tryst with a lover?"

"What?" she huffed, removing the leaves one at a time. "No. I lost my way and saw the lights. This is the first town I've seen in days." It was partially true. She hadn't seen a town since she entered the concrete box. "Where am I?"

Both his brows rose as he straightened, stroking his chin. "I believe ya *have* come a ways. Tis a strange accent ya have there. What brings ya to County Caven?"

She blinked at the man. *Where the hell is County Caven?* His intent stare had her batting her eyelashes, hoping it would distract him from asking more questions. "Which one do you prefer? The light?" She glanced over her shoulder. "Or the dark and mysterious?"

A delightful grin spread across his face. He took her by surprise draping an arm over her shoulders and turning toward the safe pub. "Tis more a matter of adventure. Do ya play it safe and go where it's warm, cozy, and predictable? Or..." He spun them both around facing the dark and mysterious. "Do ya take yer chances and have the time of yer life?"

*He does smell good and the warmth of the cloak is nice.* "I-I..."

"The time of yer life it is!" He commandeered her toward the dark and mysterious pub. The closer she got, the more it transformed into dirty and seedy.

*It'll be okay. There's Alamir everywhere—families no less.*

The young man held the door open for her. "Welcome, milady. You'll never be the same after this fair night."

She stepped into a tiny foyer where her new companion removed his cloak, hanging it on a hook, linked his arm with hers and valiantly escorted her into another world. The warm interior with its dimmed sconces accompanied by a blazing stone fireplace with an oversized wood mantle set in the middle of the room and candlelight at each table embraced her within its golden glow. A lively band filled the air with magical tunes from their fiddles, guitars, and a harmonica. Her face must have shown her surprised delight.

His lips hovered at her ear. "Not all things are as they first appear." He took her hand in his and led her past the raging fire to a table littered with glasses, some half full, others empty, and a barmaid dispersing fresh glasses of varying colors of brews—blond, golden honey, and some dark as coffee—surrounded by the biggest smiles she'd seen in a long while.

"Ronan!" A large-bellied man raised his tankard. "We weren't sure if ya were gonna show."

The man at her side laughed and picked up a glass filled with the darkest brew she'd ever seen. Or she assumed it was a beer of some sort. It certainly didn't smell like coffee.

He met his friend's *'Slainte'* and downed half the glass. "Ah! There's no finer a menace than me stout little Guinness."

Everyone at the table laughed and chugged from their glasses.

"Speaking of a fine menace. Who've ya brung with ya tonight?" the large-bellied man asked.

"Ya won't believe me if I tell ya."

"Tell us anyway. Yer tales are legendary."

A light in Ronan's eyes brightened as he winked at her and faced his audience. "There I was...minding me own business walking to town when I noticed a star flash across the night sky." He waved his hand through the air as though a master artist laying a swath of paint on canvas. "Well. We all know what ya must do when ya see a falling star!"

Someone yelled, "Make a wish!"

Ronan turned toward the voice. "Aye! So as I walked, I pondered on what to wish for." He propped his chin on his fist, rolling his eyes to the delight of the group.

"Did ya wish for gold or a shiny new sword?"

"Ah, well, I did consider 'em both. Cause I didn't want to squander me one chance at a sure thing. As I was making me decision on which wish to wish for, I come across this one standing exactly where the star had crashed."

Etain bristled at the table of wide eyes staring at her. *They don't believe this bullshit, do they?*

But he wasn't done with his story. "There she stood in the middle of the road, shining so bright, I had to shield me eyes from her glorious light." He even held up his hand in his reenactment. "And I asked if she might shine less brightly so I could look upon her beautiful countenance."

Someone from the group asked, "What's a countance?"

Another tried to help. "Maybe he means countess."

"Or accountant?" offered another.

Ronan dropped his hand and frowned. "Countenance. Her face, ya bleedin' eejits. Back to me story. Well, it seems falling from the sky is a thirsty business." He grinned and winked. "She didn't have a mind to do such a thing unless I promised to escort her into this fine establishment for a tipple. And here we are."

One of the women grabbed a glass of the dark stuff and shoved it into Etain's hand. "Here ya go, Star Countess. Drink up!"

Etain looked at Ronan, beaming as though he believed his own bullshit, clearly expecting her to drink whatever she held in her hand.

*Would a star drink this stuff?*

Seeing the same ridiculous expression on all their faces, she pulled on her big girl panties, as she'd heard her brother say on many occasions. The sudden thought made her heart nosedive.

*No. Stop it. I'm here for a reason—to find new Alamir so Sid and Angel can find me and get back to learning what I need so I can avenge my family.*

Etain brought the glass to her lips, tried not to cringe at the creamy foam on top, and filled her mouth with what smelled faintly of coffee, chocolate and cherries. Its velvety texture was not what she expected nor was the slight taste of vanilla. Or its immediate effect.

She blinked and looked at Ronan again. "Oh, my."

Everyone at the table burst into laughter, slapping each other on the back, and raising their glasses to the little star.

Ronan clinked his glass to hers. "I said the same thing when I had me first Guinness." He ran a thumb over her top lip, removing the remnants of the foam. "Yer sure to shine for a million years."

# THROUGH THE WHITE DOORS

"We have to move on, Sid," G said from his desk. "I can't sacrifice the many for one girl. I don't care how powerful she *might* be. If she wants to hide away and sulk, so be it. I have people who want our help."

Sid leaned forward in his chair. "Come on, G. She isn't like that."

He slammed his hands on the desktop and pushed out of his seat. "Then where the hell is she?"

"Hell, man, if I knew, I'd go get her and drag her in here." Sid scratched his head. "Are you sure she couldn't get outside?"

"Has she addled your brains?" G stalked from behind the desk to distance himself from his righthand man. Otherwise, he might do something they'd both regret. "You think her power is greater than mine?"

Sid twisted out of his chair. "Not greater, different. I think she's got a power we've never seen and if we don't help her get a grip on it soon, we might lose her."

G crossed his arms over his chest and raised a brow as he stroked his chin. "I didn't get that vibe from her. Are you losing your touch or do you know something I don't?"

"Ain't nothing wrong with my touch." Sid walked toward the door. "She's not the problem. It's everyone else wanting a piece of her once they find out what she can do. The *Bok's* gonna come knocking on her door one day and it's up to us to make sure she's ready to fight 'em off."

"Where you going?"

"I'm going outside to look."

"It won't do any good. We've moved locations since she went missing."

Sid stopped at the door and pursed his lips. "Then you better get us back to wherever the hell we were."

"Not until we pick up the next batch." G returned to his desk. "They've entered a bad area in the South American sector. They won't last the night if left on their own."

Sid narrowed his eyes. "Damn you. Get the goddamned coordinates set. Me, Angel, and Jacob'll take a team out and round 'em up. Once it's done, if you don't pay up, I'll get in touch with your brother and have him find her."

G huffed as he sat in his chair, shaking his head. "No need to get nasty. The sooner you get the newbs here, the sooner we can get back."

"The sooner you get a clue about what she can mean to the Alamir, the sooner your life'll get easier." He slammed the door on his way out.

"Hmph. Call my brother. What interest would he have in an Alamir?" G punched a button on his desk bringing to life a holographic map of the Alamir realm. "Hmm. Coordinates. Coordinates." He scribbled a few notes and closed it down, muttering as he stood, "She better be worth it."

Prepared to meet with Sid and G to plan their search for the new Alamir, Angel opened her door and was surprised by Isobel, standing with her fist raised.

"Isobel. What're you doing here?"

She lowered her hand. "Hi, Angel. Can I come in? It's not something I want to—"

Angel pulled her into the apartment and closed the door. "Is it Etain?"

"Well, yes."

Her heart beat in double time. "What is it?"

Isobel furrowed her brows. "Only that I haven't seen her since yesterday." Angel staggered against the wall, her hand on her chest, trying to catch a breath. Isobel reached for her and gave her a steady hand. "How about we sit down?"

She nodded and allowed the girl to guide her to the sofa. "Thank you. Why did you come here?"

Isobel sat next to her. "Her pack and sword are still in her room. She doesn't go anywhere without them."

"Have mercy. You're right. She came here last night but didn't have her sword." Angel stood. "Isobel, she might be in serious trouble."

"Why? She has to be here somewhere."

"Not necessarily."

"What do you mean?"

*Dare I trust this girl? Do I have a choice?* "What we say here stays between us. Understand?"

"Yes."

"I swear, Isobel." It was all she could do to keep herself focused on the here and now. "If I hear one word spoken about this from anyone, you're out with no recommendations or a way back."

Isobel came to her feet. "I'm worried for her, too, Angel. I won't betray her or you."

Angel closed her eyes for a moment. "I believe she's outside."

"The building? Did she find a key?"

"She didn't need one. The only way I can describe it is she has the power to travel with a mere thought."

The young woman turned away for a few moments. When she turned back, she asked, "Is she the one you and Sid brought in the night we were locked in our rooms?"

Angel considered evading the question with another. *You've spilled the tea about her power. What does it matter when she got here?* "Yes. We brought her here hoping G could help her."

Isobel was quick with her decision. "We have to find her."

Standing still was out of the question. Angel needed to be in motion, to breathe, even if it was only walking across the room. "There are others, fresh transitions, in a dangerous situation. We have innocents to save in South America."

Conviction glowed in Isobel's eyes as she moved toward her. "Give me access to the outside. I'll take a team and find her."

Angel shook her head. "We aren't there anymore. G's moved the complex."

Isobel froze. "*Moved* the complex? Where the hell are we?"

Angel rubbed her fingers across her forehead and walked away from the girl. "For the moment, we're in North Wales."

"Where's Etain?"

She stopped and faced her. "I believe she's in Ireland."

"North or south?"

Impressed by her ability to think rationally, Angel didn't hesitate. "We were in the Dún a Ri forest about five hours south of the Northern Ireland border. You'll need to get to Holyhead and take the ferry to Dublin. It's the closest port to Kingscourt."

Isobel raised a brow. "How do you know she's in Kingscourt?"

"I don't but it's the closest town."

Isobel closed the gap between them and gave her a hug. "We'll find her. How far is Holyhead from here?"

"It's a good day's walk to the west. Once you're in Dublin, it'll take another few days to get to Kingscourt. Are you sure you want to do this?"

"How can we not? She's a part of us." Isobel held her face in her hands. "But we can't get outside without your help, and it must be now. If we go to South America, who knows what we'll come back to."

Tears in her eyes, she nodded. "Get your things together. The door underneath the stairs will be open. You cannot let anyone see you leave or come back. Can I trust you?"

Isobel touched her forehead to Angel's. "We will bring her back. I promise."

⁕

Etain pushed her chair away from the table but kept her hands on the wooden surface to steady herself. "I'm gonna step outside for some air."

Ronan downed his drink and stood with her. "Charmin' idea, milady. I'll join ya."

Happy to be free of the confines of the pub, she breathed in the fresh air as she exited through the door. "It gets pretty warm in there, doesn't it?"

He laughed, watching her extend her arms and twirl several times. "I'd not noticed."

She stumbled to a stop and grinned. "Of course not. You're too busy drinking and laughing to sweat."

Leaning against the wall, he crossed his arms over his chest. "Ya have a distinctive laugh, milady. One I'm certain I heard several times. Along with a stack of empty pints in front of ya."

She placed her hands on her hips. "Well, you *were* sitting right next to me. But..." She staggered most gracefully toward him. "I didn't drink *all* those pints. I strategically enjoyed the first sip and set each glass far enough away so someone else might mistake the drink as their own. It seems to have worked a charm."

He gave her a good eyeing up and down. "Yet, ya still seem to have imbibed enough to be a bit tipsy."

"I think I'm doing pretty good for never having drank the stuff." She frowned and placed a hand over her stomach. The other hand covered her mouth as she dashed to the corner of the building.

Ronan chuckled. "And enough to possibly never drink again. Are ya all right?"

She held up a hand as another bout came over her. After a good spit, she straightened and thankfully accepted a glass of water Ronan shoved at her.

"This will help."

A gulp and another spit cleared her mouth. A splash cleansed her face. She handed the partly empty glass to the man. "That's better."

"Not quite." He raised a brow and grab a length of her hair, pouring the remainder of the water down its length. "*That's* better." He took hold of her arm to keep her steady. "Why don't ya have a sit until yer feeling less wobbly? I'll grab me cloak to keep us warm."

Etain sat on the curb. Ronan joined her not long after and draped a cloak over her shoulders. "Won't someone be looking for this later?"

His own cloak in place, he sat beside her. "Tis a small town. They'll get it back soon enough."

"It's colder than I thought. Thank you. Sorry for the—"

"Theatrics?" Ronan laughed, shaking his head. "Tis an acquired skill drinking the Guinness. It's a strong drink for a beginner. Ya should've said something."

She ran a hand through her hair, shoving it to the other side of her head and nudged her shoulder against his. "And lose what little credibility I might have?"

"They're a good lot. Most of 'em learned the same way. Trial and error."

"I gotta admit, I wasn't too sure about the place. It's so dark on the outside."

Ronan glanced over his shoulder. "Aye. We like it. It keeps the high and mighty out of our hair. Families and the upper crust go across the road." He tilted his head to the well-lit pub.

Etain's stomach constricted at the thought of the families together, sharing a meal and their lives. Warm, safe, and happy. With a shake of her head, she forced herself to focus on others who might be less fortunate than her. "Is that where new Alamir might go?"

He propped his elbows on his knees. "I expects so. Are ya looking for someone?"

Not ready to share her plan, she shrugged. "No. I just want to help newbies find their place and match them with a good clan."

"Hmm." He narrowed his eyes as he peered at her from over his arm. "Are ya here recruiting fer yer own clan?"

She swallowed having not considered what it would entail. "I don't have a clan. But I know how it feels to be new and unsure of what to do or where to go and be rejected."

He frowned thoughtfully. "I can't imagine *you* being rejected. Ya must've met some real gobshites. Do ya have connections with the clans in these parts?"

She rested her head on her knees. "No."

"Well, then," he stretched his legs out in front of him and leaned back on his hands, "would ya be in the market for a partner? Someone who *does* have connections?"

She lifted her head. "Really? You know someone who would help?"

"Aye. Tis a fine lad, indeed."

"When can I meet him? Is he in the pub?"

"Ock. No. The wee lad is busy entertaining a beautiful star. Perhaps tomorrow he might be free." His grin seemed to mock her.

The hair on her arms rose. She frowned, furrowing her brows. "Are you laughing at me?"

His back straightened and cheeks flushed red. "I am not. Tis but a wee bit of fun. Ya need to relax, milady. Yer in safe hands."

Knocking the cockiness from his demeanor eased her sudden offense but she wasn't completely convinced. "Hmph."

"Tis the truth." He nudged her shoulder with his. "Do ya have a plan?"

"No." They sat in silence for a few minutes.

Ronan's face brightened. "What if whilst yer here, ya get a job at the other pub? It's the perfect place to meet any newbs who come into town. They won't dare come over here since, as you said, it has a sinister persona."

She rolled her eyes. "I said it was dark and mysterious, but do you think they'd hire me?"

"Hard to say. Do ya have experience working in a pub?"

"Not a pub but my mom was a bartender, and I helped her sometimes."

"I think yer prospects are good. Why don't ya go in the morning and ask?"

Her shoulders drooped, glancing up and down the street. She'd forgotten her predicament. "In the *morning*?"

Ronan pushed up to his feet. "Excellent! It's settled."

"Hmph." *Maybe I can find a place to tuck into.*

He cocked his head. "Where ya staying?"

She didn't want to meet his gaze, afraid he would see the uncertainty in her eyes. "I-I hadn't—"

He grabbed her by the arm and pulled until she stood. "Ya can stay with me and me clan for as long as ya need. We have plenty of room and you'll be safe and warm. Ya don't want to be on the streets on a cold night around here, milady."

"Why would you do that? We just met."

"And shared many a brew." He leaned toward her. "I've seen ya at yer worst, haven't I? And I'm still here. You'll be a lot safer with us." He seemed to sense her hesitation. "We're just beyond the edge of town. If ya don't like what ya see, yer free to walk away. Won't anyone make ya stay."

*It's gotta be better than sleeping outside.* "Okay."

He linked arms with her as they walked along the cobbled road. His big grin made her feel better about her decision bringing on a sudden thought. "If I get the job tomorrow, what am I gonna do about finding clans for the newbs?"

He patted her hand. "You bring 'em in, me darlin', and I'll find 'em a home."

It didn't take long to reach the end of the lit cobbled road. Etain moved a little closer to her companion as they walked into the darkness and first drops of a fresh rain. "'Tis a bit down the road. You'll see the lights soon."

The further they walked, the more she doubted her decision to go with the handsome young man. But, once again, twinkling lights in the distance silenced her fears. "There she is. The little castle we call home."

As they came closer, the lights were set farther apart than what they'd appeared from afar, and as a result, she couldn't tell much about the building itself except it seemed bigger than what she would call little. Her boots clattered against the wooden slats of the bridge to the main entrance. A pair of great medieval style metal doors creaked open at their approach.

They were met by four large men wrapped head to boots in hooded raincoats with what resembled a mini cape across the shoulders. Initially, they reminded her of the ranchers back home but with their grunts and rough handling she decided maybe they edged more toward the serial killers she'd seen in the movies.

She assumed they were Ronan's clan mates. It was hard to tell. There were no friendly greetings or handshakes or even shared smiles between the men. Exchanged grunts had them through the gates and into the main keep where the lighting wasn't much better. She thought it odd considering the camaraderie she'd seen within other clans, not that they'd shared it with her. But these men didn't seem to be mates at all.

Ronan took hold of her elbow and guided her toward and through the main doors of the castle. "Never mind the grumpy guards. They don't take kindly to having their quiet nights disturbed. Let's get ya to a room."

Etain pulled free from his grip. The foyer was what she expected—gray, cavernous, and intimidating—split in half by a huge stone stairway leading up to another floor. The stairs were not pretty or inspiring or gracious. *Utilitarian.* She breathed in and forced a smile on her face with the hope it would keep the wolves at bay. *Wolves? Stop it, Etain. You're Alamir. Stop being a baby.* "Where's the rest of the clan? Do I get to meet any of them? Shouldn't we tell someone we're here?"

"'Tis late, milady. Ya can meet 'em in the morning." He reached for her, but she stepped away.

As a ploy to delay the trip up the foreboding stairs, she changed the subject. "What's the name of your clan?"

His shoulders slumped as he lowered his hand. "Etain. Tis been a long day. I'd like to be in me own bed a few hours before the morning comes and have to tend me duties."

She had to admit he didn't look as fresh as he had earlier in the evening. *Maybe he's older than I thought.* "Duties?"

He lowered his head with sigh and rubbed his red-rimmed eyes several times. "Checking the perimeter, making sure the livestock's fed and watered, and other things needed doing on a clan estate. We try to be as self-sufficient as possible."

She bit her bottom lip as he placed a foot on the first step. "Oh. I hadn't thought about that."

"Great. Now can we—"

"At least, tell me the name of your clan."

He peered over his shoulder. "Does it matter?"

A determined Etain shifted on her feet. "If you expect me to stay here tonight, yes."

Ronan faced her; his lips pressed together. "TNP—Take No Prisoners."

Her throat went dry, making it difficult to swallow. Not a name she recognized, but it left the impression intended. "Okay. Thank you."

At the top of the stairs, he turned right and followed the hallway until it ended at a pair of tall white doors covered in carvings of vines, leaves, and flowers and sporting shiny brass handles. Ronan pulled an exotic gold key from the folds of his cloak, opened the doors, and stepped inside.

"Ya can stay here fer the night. There's a bathing room over there." His head tilted in the general direction.

Etain stood at the doors, perusing the immense room. A beautiful canopy draped from the ceiling above an oversized bed created the illusion of a four-poster. The head and foot boards were carved from a black stone or maybe wood? The bedding in silvers and blacks added to the masculine feel of the room but the canopy and soft, shiny fabrics softened it with a feminine flair.

"I can sleep on a sofa. Really. I don't need this."

He spun on his heels. "No. Yours truly will sleep better knowing yer safe behind a locked door. Some clan members tend to—wander at night."

"Hmm. Seems to be pathological," she muttered more to herself.

"I'm serious." He damn near stomped toward her at the door, grabbed her by the arm, and pulled her in.

Unsure of what to think, she stood dumbfounded, watching him step into the hallway and close the doors.

With a roll of her eyes, she sighed and dragged her feet to the door until the bloody key clicked in the lock. "What the fuck?" Panic set her heart beating too fast, the blood rushing through her as though a dam had broken, yet she managed to keep her voice steady. "Open the door, Ronan."

She barely heard his muffled response. "I'll see ya in the morning."

The coolness of the handles sent shivers through her as she tested them despite what he'd done. "Open the fucking door."

"Tomorrow."

Her hand slammed against the white wood. "No! Open this goddamn door." She stumbled back, staring at her hand. *Was that a blue flash? Crap, Etain. Keep your shit straight.* She returned to the door. "Hello? Are you there?"

"Get to bed. I'll be seeing ya in the morning."

She twisted around, pressing her back to the door; and shoved her hands under her arms. "Don't count on it."

# A LITTLE VAVOOM

Ronan bared his teeth as he pushed from the door and stalked back the way he'd come. At the landing, he was surprised by a fellow clan member, who seemed to have nothing better to do than stick his bleedin' nose into his business. "Tenant. How long ya been standing there?"

The bald man was not as tall as him but could be as intimidating with his broad shoulders and a set of unnerving gray eyes that saw everything a person tried to hide. He grinned as he shrugged. "Yer looking a bit peaked there. She's not what ya thought, is she?"

Ronan raised a brow. "Yer full of shite, old man."

Tenant laughed. "Not so old I can't enjoy meself with a tasty morsel like her."

"Hmph. It's been a long day and tomorrow doesn't look any better."

He winked a gleeful eye. "Ya left her alone. Untouched." He leaned toward him. "In *your* room."

A cold sweat trickled down his back. Ronan growled, baring his teeth again. "Go to bed, Tenant. I feel the morning comin'."

"Cool yer jets, boyo." Tenant stepped toward him, giving him a not so complimentary once over. "Remember, we share in this clan, no matter how pretty the bounty. Take yer piece and bring her to me. Then ya can sell her to the *Bok* and move on to the next one. They love 'em broken."

Both men had experienced the brutality of the *Bok* firsthand. A run in with the brutes several years ago ended with half the clan slaughtered and their own heads on the chopping block. Ronan with his silver tongue, negotiated terms to spare the lives of those left alive and provide a steady income.

His survival and that of the clan rested on a tenuous agreement to deliver a constant flow of fresh Alamir. The *Bok* didn't care about the who, the what, or the why. Give 'em a proper body to corrupt and they'd do the rest. But above all, the product had to be salvageable in mind and body. The spirit didn't matter.

An unexpected anger lit his blood on fire. *Startin' a fight with this one won't end well for any of us. Like he said, cool yer jets.* Ronan swallowed and gave the man a suave smile. "This one's gonna take a wee bit more finesse. If she breaks too hard, too fast, the *Bok* won't pay for what's left." Noting the hardness in the gray eyes, he turned to the stairs, happy to see he'd struck a nerve. He glanced over his shoulder. "Ya best remember tis me who has the relationship."

The hardness shifted into what Ronan interpreted as understanding.

Tenant gave his best bluster. "Just remember what I said."

Ronan chuckled as he headed down. "Oh, aye. I shan't forget." At the bottom of the stairs, he found the closest empty room, locking the door once inside. "Fucking hell. I should've left her in town."

A snap of his fingers brought a fire to life in the fireplace as he pulled his cloak close, threw himself on a Chesterfield sofa, and closed his eyes. But his brain wouldn't shut down. Scenario after scenario played through his head, none of them ending well for Etain. His eyes popped open. "I don't understand why I give a shit, but I've got to get her out. Tonight."

Etain slid down the door and jammed her hands into her hair, resting her elbows on her knees. "Calm down. I'm in here and he's out there." She lifted her head, clasping her hands together.

"He has the key and can come in any time he wants." She pushed up from the floor. "I have to secure the door until *I'm* ready for someone to come in."

To her right stood a wall-to-wall wardrobe as black as the bed with four pairs of doors. One set held men's shirts and trousers. The next was filled with cloaks and dusters. Another held hats, boots and shoes. The last had an array of belts, leather straps, drawers of cuff links, necklaces, head pieces, and a few items she wasn't sure what they were for. Those items she didn't touch. "Is this...*his* room? Or is someone else waiting for the key? Shit, I gotta get out of here."

Drawn to the leather belts, she grabbed two of the heaviest ones, a handful of leather straps, and returned to the doors. "If they want in here, they're gonna have to work for it."

She wrapped a few of the leather straps around and around one handle and looped it to the other going around and around again and finished it off with the tail in a knot. She did the same with the other belt, its looped knot at the opposite handle. The remaining straps she used to bind all the pieces together. One more trip to the wardrobe for a few more belts and the intricate leather masterpiece was complete.

Etain admired her handiwork. "It won't hold for long, but they won't be sashaying in whenever they please either."

The room had so many possibilities. *Secret panels? Windows? Could there be a hidden staircase?* Her survey of the room was more meticulous this time running her fingers along panel edges, checking full length mirrors, and draperies. No hidden passages, mirrored doors, or windows big enough to wiggle through.

"Snug as a bug," she whispered, sitting on the edge of the bed, eyeing the room again. "Come on, it's a castle. There has to be another way out of this room." The opening to the bathing room caught her eye. "Oh. Hey. Maybe the vanity swivels into another room?" Off the bed in an instant, she laughed walking into the tiled room. Nothing seemed off or out of place.

*I've never seen a tub in the middle of a room. Interesting.* The black and silver scheme continued with a black toilet and tub. Double black sinks sat underneath two large silver-framed mirrors atop a silver vanity. While the walls were covered in black tiles, the floor was silver-gray wood planks. But the taps, handles, and towels were gold.

"Weird. Hmm. Now I'm in here, I *do* need to pee." On the toilet, what appeared to be an irregularity in the flooring had her leaning to the side for a better perspective. She finished her business and flushed, quickly pulling up her jeans, and stared at the floor around the tub while she washed her hands.

Crouched next to the tub, she ran a finger along a dark line wider than the other lines in the tile. "Is that a gap? Or a flaw?" The edges were distinct, and the pad of her finger dipped into a tiny space along the full length of the tub. She noticed how the planks didn't match up at the end. Nor did they match at the head of the tub.

She leaned back on her hands, emitting a small laugh, placed her feet on the side of the tub, and pushed. With little effort, the vessel slid sideways, revealing a set of spiral stairs. "Aha! I wonder how far down they go." She ducked her head into the black hole but didn't see much. "Well, there's only one way to know."

In the wee hours of the morning, after everyone had retired, Isobel, Roxy, and Tristan met in Etain's room.

Isobel pulled her hair into a tail and secured it with a band. "I'm sorry I couldn't give you more notice. If we don't leave now, we'll be stuck in a place where we can't get to her."

Roxy checked her bag one more time and slipped it onto her back. "Etain needs our help. I'm glad you included me."

Tristan adjusted the straps for his scabbard across his chest. "Yeah. The sooner we get her back, the better. I can't believe we left her."

Isobel's eyes widened. "I can't believe we were in Ireland. You've kept this to yourselves, right?"

"Yeah," Tristan said, exchanging a glance with Roxy, "but do you think it's smart just the three of us going?"

Isobel slipped her pack onto her shoulder. "Unless you want G breathing down our necks. I hope with so many newbs coming in, he won't notice us missing. He'd definitely notice if more went."

Roxy walked to the door. "Let's go. Didn't you say Angel wouldn't leave it open for long?"

Isobel followed. "Tristan, can you carry Etain's pack? She'll be wanting her sword."

"I got it."

Without a sound, the three made their way to the landing where Etain had spent her first night in the complex and down the stairs, heads turning to make sure they weren't followed, listening for the slightest sound. At the last step, they slipped underneath the stairs, located the metal door and ever so gently opened it.

Tristan waited until the girls were a good ten feet away, closed the door, hearing he lock click, and ran to catch up. When he glanced over his shoulder one last time, the complex was gone. The three reassured each other with a group huddle and disappeared into the night.

Ronan stepped out of the room into the dimly lit foyer. A good sign everyone had finally slipped off to bed. Still, his senses were on high alert for any signs of life aside from his.

Tenant had abandoned his perch at the top of the stairs. *Thank fuck.* Ronan checked the area to be sure and turned toward the double white doors. From where he stood, nothing seemed to be out of sorts, yet he held his breath until he stood in front of them. No signs of an attempted break in or break out. Things were going well.

After another look over his shoulder, he pulled the golden key from his cloak, inserted it into the keyhole, and turned until it clicked. He stashed the key into his cloak and placed each hand on a shiny brass handle, the cold of the metal warming at his touch. The handles turned easily enough but the doors didn't budge.

With a furrowed brow, he tried again using more force. The doors gave in somewhat. "What the hell?" This time, he put his shoulder to it. Although there was a little more give, still the doors wouldn't open. But there was a gap. Ronan pressed an eye to the opening. "Etain. What're ya playing at? Open the door, girl."

He pushed with his shoulder again and again until he realized the resistance wasn't from something blocking the doors. It was as if they were attached to one another. Ronan stepped back, eyeing the opening from top to bottom, and crouched for a closer inspection. There seemed to be an obstruction at the handles.

"Are those... Are those me bloody belts?" He popped up, reaching for his sword. "Ya wicked wee wench. Clever, but wicked."

With a single slice, the sharp edge cut straight through. Freed from the leather bondage, the doors easily opened with a slight push. "Yer gonna replace those, milady."

He checked the room, the bed, and the wardrobe, in case she was hiding, and finally headed into the bathing room. "Holy mother of..." He flew down the winding stairs with an insane hope she hadn't run into anyone. Especially Tenant. "Killing a clan mate is not a good way to start me day."

At the bottom step, a sound outside the door made him stop. He pictured the dark hallway on the other side with doors to all parts of the castle. He knew how to get to the foyer, but she didn't. A muffled grunt set him into a careful, quiet motion.

* * *

A disgusting old man had one leg between hers, his hard, sweaty body pressing her into the stone wall, and his grubby hand over her mouth. She couldn't maneuver a knee into his groin, as much as she wanted to, or reach for the dagger in her boot. Hell, she could hardly move at all. *You fuck twat.*

Once her eyes adjusted to the bit of light in the large space, she made out his leer and if she weren't in such a compromised position, thanks to him, she might have thought him somewhat tolerable to look at. Not handsome but not disgusting except for his other hand grazing along her side, groping up to her breast. *Totally gross.*

A breath passed her lips in a long, hard wheeze. Sparks set her brain on fire as anger fed a desire to smash his face. A random memory of watching Felix the Cat reruns ran through her mind. *If only I could scream like little Vavoom. I'd splatter you all over this stupid castle.* "Let me go."

His grin made her want to puke but he moved his hand from her mouth.

"I'll be letting ya go once ya pay fer yer stay."

"I wouldn't be here if you'd get the fuck off me."

"Interesting choice of word. Fuck. Puts me mind right at ease." His other hand went to her crotch. "If ya do me right, maybe I won't be selling ya to the *Bok* after all."

Unable to hold in a gasp at the affront, her cheeks burned, and stomach rolled. This type of behavior she'd never experienced in her short life. Her heart beat too fast, the blood rushing to her head. *Shit, what's he doing now?* She watched him grapple at his belt but wasn't sure what to do to stop whatever was about to happen.

A small voice inside broke through the fog. *You've seen a naked boy. You've heard the nasty stories at school. Remember the things you saw in the library?*

His hard mouth assaulted hers, suffocating and gritty, his stone tongue driving down her throat. The neckline of her t-shirt burned her skin as it gave way. She pushed as hard as she could, trying to knee his groin. The sound of a zipper drove her to near madness.

*No! Not you! Not here!* screamed in her head, but only a hiss passed her lips.

Before the small voice had the chance to speak again, she grabbed the man by the balls.

"Oh, yeah. Just the way I—"

And squeezed with all her might.

The smile faded from his grimy lips. His eyes bulged. The invasive hands fell away from her, reaching for her hand as she forced him back, directing him with his balls. His cock fell limp over her wrist. She pushed him back across the hall, squeezing with all her might.

*You have the power. Use it! Fry his limp dick into crackling.*

Once she had him pinned against the opposing wall, her hand lit in a blue flash, zapping his privates with electrical pulses. His screams echoed throughout the hallway. She leaned into his twisted face. "Can't eat the shit you dish out, can you?"

A force rammed into her, grabbing at her, and yelling but she didn't let go of the cry-baby man. "Etain!"

Ronan's voice. Her head turned in time to see the fist headed toward her. In the next moment, rain pelted her head and shoulders. *Outside. On the main road. Safe from the monsters inside. Get out of here.* Fortunately, the cloak Ronan had given her at the pub still sat on her shoulders. She pulled the hood over her head and ran in the direction she'd come from earlier.

The cold darkness and relentless rain merely enforced her determination to locate as many new Alamir as she could and steer them away from this awful place.

"How many have they raped and sold to the *Bok*?" She pulled the cloak closer, diverting her desire to crumple to the ground into constructive daydreams. Determination propelled each step, keeping her warm and focused on what she would do next. "If I can't find decent clans to take them, I'll start my own. We'll search out other clans like this one and destroy them."

Unable to see more than a step or two in front of her, she stumbled into an unseen puddle and nearly nosedived into another. Thanks to her audacious boots and some fancy footwork, she saved herself. She had to stay on her feet and keep moving. The further she got away from this place, the better.

Although, killing the creeps *would* be a comforting salve to her bruised sense of right and wrong. Could she do it? Would she?

# KANIA

Eventually, lights twinkled in the distance. She walked straight to the pub of light but its large windows told her everything. The doors were locked and the lights turned off. With a sigh, she plopped down on the stoop, looked right, left, and ended with her narrowed sights on the pub across the road. Maybe it was closed, maybe not. It was hard to tell with the entire thing painted black. "I'll never set foot in there again and neither will new Alamir."

Perusing the building itself, she noticed a glow in a window on the upper floor and stood, remembering that some pubs had rooms to rent. "If they have them..." She stepped into the road, turning to survey the pub behind her. Sure enough, there were windows above. *But the doors are locked. Maybe there's a side or rear entrance for guests?*

A gap between the pub and the building next door gave her hope. Upon investigation, a streetlight at the other end confirmed it was a walkway, and without further consideration, she stepped onto the path. Halfway down, she discovered a dimly lit door, so dim it wasn't noticeable from the street. Upon her approach, the bulb brightened.

She reached for the handle but hesitated and pulled back. *Is this stupid or brave? Listening to Ronan and going with him was stupid. Standing here in the rain is stupid. So, odds are this is brave, or at least less stupid. I'm going for a positive outlook and consider it brave. As long as I don't get caught.*

She turned the handle and quietly stepped into a tiny foyer to a set of stairs winding over her head and a small reception area tucked in the space underneath. No one seemed to be around, so she lifted the hinged part of the counter and slipped into an office big enough for a desk and chair.

A box nailed to the wall above the desk held exactly what she needed—keys. There were six hooks—three on the top row and three beneath. Two on top and one below were empty. Each key had its own blue tag emblazoned with a golden number—two, five, and six sparkled in the dim light. She grabbed number five.

Up the stairs in record time, she found the corresponding room halfway between the end of the hall and the stairway. A jiggle of the key and flick of a light switch, she was in a plain room with what looked to be a cozy bed. "It's all I need."

Walking deeper into the room, she laid the key on a table that doubled as a desk, grabbed the chair, and wedged it underneath the door handle. "No more creepies tonight."

She removed the cloak and draped it over a worn easy chair in the corner next to a radiator beneath a window, checked the thermostat and ramped it up to eighty, delighted by the sudden heat. Once the initial chill subsided, she headed into the bathroom.

In the mirror, a dirty, tearstained face stared at her. "When was I crying?" Her hair was worse. "A shower would be good."

While the water warmed, she removed her boots and every stitch of clothing, washing everything as best she could. A laddered radiator in the bathroom served as the perfect spot for her wet clothes and boots to dry.

Washed, refreshed, and wrapped in a large white towel, she grabbed another to dry her hair and picked up her jeans, laying them over the radiator in the room. A quick perusal of the goodie tray revealed her dining pleasure for the evening. *Shortbread and tea for supper or ginger cookies and hot chocolate?*

Partially filling the kettle with water, she set it on the warming plate, ripped open a hot chocolate packet and dumped it into a cup. "Ginger with tea in the morning and shortbread tonight with my cocoa."

Warm and cozy in the bed, she set her delights on the side table and fluffed her pillows to the perfect puff. Try as she might to consume the shortbread in a ladylike manner, once the buttery piece of heaven crumbled into her mouth, it was over. The hot chocolate served as the perfect after dinner drink. Not long after, her eyes closed.

A knock on the door and jiggling of the handle woke her. "Shit!" Her first instinct was to glance at the window. Daylight shone at the edges of the curtains. "Shit! What time is it?" She threw off the covers, jumped out of bed, and dashed into the bathroom for a quick pee, dressed, and shoved the ginger snaps and packets of tea into her pockets.

At the door, she heard someone say, "Let's find the manager. Maybe there's been a mix up in rooms." Followed by fading footsteps.

Etain moved the chair aside and slowly opened the door. Alone in the hallway, except for a housekeeping cart at the next room, she closed the door and walked toward the exit, pulling the hood over her head just as a maid came from another room.

"*Maidin mhaith,*" the woman said as Etain passed.

Assuming she'd wished her a good morning, she didn't look at her but mumbled, "*Bore da.*"

She flew down the stairs, out the side door, and didn't stop running until she stood among the trees of the forest. Exhilarated by the drama, she rested against a glorious old tree, sucked in the air and laughed until she could no longer stand.

But thoughts of being alone in a foreign country with no friends or contacts soon dampened the laughing frenzy. "Man. What a mess." She pushed up onto her feet, gathered her hair in her hands, braided the thick mane, and knotted the ends. "We're gonna find shelter. Then we're gonna walk this forest until we either find new Alamir or Master G's stupid complex returns."

Etain spent most of her first days avoiding Ronan, who seemed compelled to hunt her down, although she was certain he had no clue she was there. Day after day, his dogged determination forced her deeper and deeper into the forest, which led her to the river, an important water source, and a ruin of four stone walls in various stages of decay draped in ivy. The canopy above provided an organic ceiling of branches and leaves so tightly knit they kept out most of the rain yet cast a warm glow over the structure.

A few days later, it was as though Ronan no longer existed. Although she'd not seen hide nor hair of the man, her senses remained on high alert—just in case. Every crack of a twig or rustle of leaves had her ducking into the brush or hiding behind a tree. Eventually, her nerves settled and while she paid attention to unusual sounds, she no longer ran for cover. But the dagger in her boot was either in her hand or not far from it.

Unsure of how long she might be stranded, she constructed a fire pit, clearing the grasses and undergrowth in the driest quarter of her base and spent hours gathering anything she thought would burn—sticks, leaves, and bits of bark. Her next feat was to create fire.

Thinking back to the days when she and her family would go camping, she found a large flat stone among those fallen from the walls of the old castle, setting it close to the fire pit. From her pile of larger sticks, she tested several, searching for a softwood, one that dented easily with a nail, and used her dagger to dig into the wood forming a shallow circle. She chose a somewhat smaller but longer stick for her spindle, knocked off any protrusions, and cut off one end for a smooth, flat surface. With the end of the spindle in the circle, she rolled it between her hands a few times, making it deeper, carved a notch at the edge, and lodged the driest piece of bark underneath the notch.

With the flat stick held in place by her foot, she spit on her hands, and started at the top, rolling the spindle between her hands working down its length. Over and over, she repeated the process. Just as a small trail of smoke wafted from the piece of bark, the spindle broke in her hands. "Damn it."

She grabbed another stick and started the process again. "I'm not freezing my ass off another night." The spindle broke again. "Come on! I used to do this all the time."

Memories of her first night in the Alamir brought to mind the blue flashes she created slapping her hand against the brick of the building where the Gathering had been held. And the toilet stall she destroyed the next day. "Could it work?" Shifting onto her knees, she piled a handful of tinder onto the stone slab. "If anger is what it takes, get mad. Get real mad."

She had plenty. From the loss of her family to what she'd endured since, her breath quickened, and her jaws clenched. A warm flush tingled over her scalp, traveling the length of her body. Every word spoken against her. Every mistreatment she'd endured. Even the horror of thinking she'd murdered a friend came to the torture party; the final piece being Ronan's betrayal. *Was he watching from the dark while that shit molested me? Was he waiting for his turn?*

"You son of a bitch! I trusted you." She stood, balling her hands into fists. "You didn't do anything until your bastard friend was in trouble."

A guttural scream came from deep inside her as she clawed at the ivy on the stone walls, organic confetti falling to the ground. "Asshole!" A kick to the wall fired the ivy into a blue flame. "He was gonna sell *me* to the *Bok*? *After* he raped me." She ran a hand through her hair. "And Ronan didn't do a goddamn thing. Not for me. How many others has he done this to?" She kicked another wall, lighting its trailing ivy.

A new realization made her stumble backward. "Holy shit. Was it his plan all along? I bring them in, and he sells them to the *Bok*? If they're lucky enough to not get raped before the handover." She paced back and forth, banging her fists against the walls, setting fire to everything clinging to the stones. "Fuck! Fuck! *Fuck!* What an idiot. You gotta wise up, girl. If it comes easy, it's bullshit." She sucked in ragged, slow breaths. "You're gonna regret ever messing with me."

She staggered, marveling at the fires, and cringed at the growing ache in her head. Lightheaded and exhausted, she grabbed a wad of tinder and set it ablaze before placing it in the fire pit. Visions of a castle engulfed in flames brought a smile to her lips as she stacked sticks around her blue flame.

<hr>

Etain woke in the same spot where she had collapsed. One eye opened and closed at the bright light of the morning. She rolled onto her back, laying an arm over her eyes. *Thank goodness the headache is gone.* But frowned at the disgusting taste in her mouth, sticking out her tongue as though the fresh air of the day would cleanse away the nasties. *Ugh. I need water.*

"*Guten morgen. Ich bin froh, dass du libst.*"

Her heart froze for an instant and the hairs on her head stood on end. "What?" She shifted, turning her head, and pushed up into a sitting position. A handsome, somewhat older man with a bushy mustache sat cross-legged next to the firepit, adding sticks to a bigger flame, his longish dark brown curls framing a set of inquisitive green eyes.

*At least it isn't Ronan.*

His clothing wasn't what she'd come to expect of Alamir issue—leather or costumery—except for his jacket. *Well, Etain, you're in jeans and a t-shirt. Maybe his transition was different.*

She ran her hands through her hair. "Where'd you come from?"

His rosy-lipped grin revealed a perfect set of white teeth. "The last I remember was drinking an ice-cold beer with my friends."

"Was that Ronan?"

He pursed his lips still feeding the fire. "Hmph. Never heard the name."

Her eyes narrowed. "You could be lying."

"You're right," he shrugged, placing his hands on his knees, "I could but I'm not sure how to convince you otherwise."

Etain stood, dusting herself off. "I need to pee."

"Yes, ma'am."

"If you move at all, I will end you."

He kept still except for a single blink of his eyes. "We can't have that. Take care of your business. I'll be here tending this nice little fire you started."

She headed toward a grove of bushes, peed, and went to the river, washed her face and rinsed out her mouth. *Could this be my first newbie? I really don't want to kill him. But, if it comes down to me or him, he's toast.*

Returning to the enclosure, she stopped at the entrance, surprised to find the man where she'd left him. A mix of frustration and relief made her edgy. As he turned in his seat, she walked toward the firepit and plopped down opposite him. "Who are you?"

"My name is Kania."

"Were you speaking German earlier?"

"You understand German?"

"Not really. But I recognized *guten morgen*."

He accepted her explanation with a nod. "I was in Germany last night, drinking with friends, and thought perhaps I was still there. As odd as it sounds."

"I get it. I was in Texas when I transitioned and found myself in Wales. Your accent doesn't sound German."

"I was born in Germany, but we moved around through Europe, so my accent is more European." Kania considered their surroundings. "Is this Wales?"

"No. We're in Ireland."

His brows rose but his demeanor seemed to deflate. "Ireland? *Wie zum Teufel...*"

"I can't explain how it works. You're in the Alamir realm. *We* are Alamir."

He ran a finger along his jawline in thought. "What is Alamir?"

Hands in her lap, she considered where to start. "We are warriors who protect the human realm."

A crease showed between his brows. "The human *realm*? From what?"

"Evil. Demons, *Bok*, and Alamir who work with the *Bok*."

"Wait a minute." He jumped up, slicking back his curls with both hands. "I didn't think I drank that much. This has got to be a dream."

She didn't blink an eye. "If only it were."

"How the hell did I get here?"

"You tell me. It's different for everyone."

He turned away in a huff but faced her again, his face pale. "Why? Why would I be chosen? I'm not a *warrior*. I mean, I can fight if I have to, but..." He leaned over, placing his hands on his knees, panting.

Etain came to her feet and rushed to his side. "Breathe, Kania. I'll help you with your transition."

"The human *realm*?" he wheezed.

"I'm afraid so."

"Holy Mother of..." He straightened and spun on his heels as though he were leaving, panting the entire time but stopped at the wall, hands on his hips, and stood there, staring at the trees.

Etain returned to the firepit and waited, thinking it better to give him time to process rather than adding more fuel to the fire.

After several moments of shifting from side to side and shaking his head, he came back to the pit. "How long have you been...Alamir?"

"I'm not sure. Weeks, months? Time isn't measured here the same as in the human world."

He sank to the ground into a cross-legged position. "Who are you?"

"I'm Etain."

"Why are you in Ireland? Hell, why am *I* in Ireland?"

"I don't think you're ready for that yet." She watched him twitch and pick at his mustache in his struggle to come to terms with his situation. "Let's start with something easy. How did you find me?" When he didn't respond, she repeated her questions. "Kania. How did you find me?"

He smoothed his mustache and met her gaze. "I, uh, well, there was a blue glow in the trees. With it being dark, I walked toward it but by the time I arrived, there was only this flame." He nodded at the firepit. "I thought it odd until I noticed the charred walls. Was that your doing?"

She stared at the fire, rubbing her thumbs over the cuticle of each finger, flayed out her hands, and curled them into fists as she twisted her wrists, comforted by the resounding pop from each one. "I'm still coming to terms with my power."

He paled again. "P-Power?"

"My Alamir power."

"Your…" He touched his chest. "Does that mean *I* have a power?"

"I'm pretty sure you do. Don't worry, we'll figure it out."

Kania sucked in a breath and chuckled. "Is there coffee in this realm?"

"There is, but I don't have any. What I do have is a river full of clear, cold water." She stood and stretched. "Let's scrounge up some breakfast and see if we can discover the power of Kania the new Alamir."

"Breakfast? Is there a place to eat I didn't notice?"

Etain laughed, spreading her arms wide. "It's all around us. But you gotta know where to look. Unless you're willing to hunt."

"Hunt what?"

"Meat."

"Meat?"

From the expression on his face, she could practically see the wheels turning.

"Where would we find meat in this place?" The dawning of a new age shown in his wide eyes, his face gone pale again. "Oh. *Hunt*. As in prey, which would involve things I'd rather not think about."

"Which is why we eat other things. But now we have fire, so perhaps we can fish."

Kania chuckled as he stood. "Gutting a fish, I can do. Good thing this came with me." His hand disappeared under his jacket and reappeared with a serious, fixed-blade knife.

Etain swallowed and sniffed, the adrenaline pumping up the volume, but maintained a cool façade as she displayed her dagger. "Do you know what to look for?"

"Ha! I was born in a forest."

# GREAT EXPECTATIONS

"**A**re you sure of which way to go?" Tristan scratched his head staring at the mix of historic buildings and modern architecture along the waterfront of the Dublin Docklands.

Isobel shielded her eyes from the bright sunshine. "Angel said the town is north of Dublin and the forest is just beyond it."

He slung Etain's pack onto his shoulder and rubbed his gloved hands together. "Of course. It's probably even colder up there."

She laid a hand on his forearm. "At least it isn't raining. We have to find her, Tris."

"We will. I wish she'd waited until we were in South America to disappear."

Isobel smirked. "Then you'd be moaning about the sweat."

"Not me, sister. I love to sweat." He winked and led the way down the gangplank from the ferry.

Roxy caught up to them on the docks, adjusting the pack on her back. "We've been traveling for weeks. How do we know when we've gotten to where we're going?"

Tristan spoke over his shoulder. "When we run into a silver-haired tornado."

"In a forest?"

"Don't be negative, Roxy," Isobel snapped.

Tristan chastised her with a stern eye. "Don't be a bitch, Isobel. We're all you got."

Back straight, she stared ahead. "Sorry. I'm concerned, is all."

"Hey," he nudged her with a shoulder, "we'll find her. Even if we have to search the whole damn island. Have a little faith in your team."

"I'm scared for her. She does a pretty good job of acting confident, but she isn't."

Tristan narrowed his eyes. "I didn't realize you two had gotten so close."

She shrugged, giving him a hopeful smile. "I guess I've gotten a little protective of her."

Roxy poked her head in between the two. "Are we talking about the same person?"

Isobel rolled her eyes and moved back a few steps. "Yes, Roxy. She seems like a kid sometimes."

"Hmph. Does she? I haven't noticed."

Isobel glared. "Because you're starstruck."

"*I'm* starstruck? You're the one worried about her. I think she's probably doing fine."

Tristan stepped in front of Roxy, separating the two women. With a huff, she moved to his other side. "Be careful, Isobel" he said. "She doesn't strike me as the type to want protection." He leaned away from her furious glare. "I'm not saying she doesn't need it. Just don't expect gratitude."

"Shut up, Tristan." Isobel stomped ahead.

Roxy tugged on his sleeve, her eyes on the redhead. "We should back off and let her have this if only for a little while. Honesty isn't helping."

"I'm tired of seeing her heart break every time someone leaves her behind."

She tilted her head; her brows knitted in a curious manner. "What makes you think it'll happen this time?"

People shuffled past them, bumping Tristan into Roxy. He pulled her further aside. "Sorry. We're a blip in Etain's journey. She might stick around for a while, but she'll move on. Her destiny is bigger than us."

Roxy snorted a laugh. "Come on, Tris. The *chosen* one?"

"Hmph. Too cliché. But she *is* special in a way we aren't." He eyed her from the corner of his eye. "Don't ask me to explain it 'cause I can't. It's a gut thing."

Roxy grinned, squinting up at him. "Or maybe the ferry ride didn't agree with you."

He had to laugh. "Maybe so. We better get moving or we'll get left behind."

They followed the road north until it ended at a crossroads going east and west. Tristan stared across green fields dusted with a light frost. "We'll need to go this way if we plan to keep heading north."

Well into the night, without passing another town, the three called it a day, set up camp between a cropping of rocks, shared a light supper, and crashed for a few hours of sleep.

⁂

The three woke to an overcast morning, the musty smell of distant rain in the air. Tristan rose first and disappeared to take care of personal business while the girls did the same. Back at the camp, Roxy passed out chunks of bread and cheese. "Not as good as Winston's but it'll keep us going."

Tristan nodded over his shoulder. "I heard running water over there. We can freshen up and refill our canteens."

"I'll be glad to get back to daily baths and Winston's home-cooked meals," Isobel said, running her fingers through her hair.

"Sit and let me braid it for you." Roxy kneeled, motioning to Isobel.

"Thanks, Rox. Maybe it won't feel so disgusting."

Isobel plopped on the ground in front of her.

Roxy laughed. "If it's a river over there, perhaps we should all jump in and have a wash."

Tristan tore into his chunk of bread. "We'd just end up wet and smellier."

The girls laughed.

"If we catch a good wind, maybe Etain'll come looking to see what smells so bad and find us." Roxy finished off the braid in a knot.

"That would be great." Isobel stood, smoothing her hands over the braid. "Thank you, Rox. You're a star."

Tristan shoved his pack on one shoulder and Etain's on the other. "Shall we get moving? We shouldn't be too far away now."

Sometime in the early afternoon, the three came across a well-worn road. Isobel grabbed her compass to check their direction. "It's a bit curvy but it seems to be a north and south road. Shall we try it?"

"Will it take us into a town?" Roxy asked.

Tristan led the way. "Let's find out."

An hour later, the terrain turned rockier with a large ravine to the right side of the road.

Roxy shielded her eyes from the glare off the clouds and pointed. "Is it a castle?"

Tristan and Isobel did the same.

"It is. I wonder if a clan lives there." Tristan lowered his hand and continued walking.

Isobel followed, glancing at the structure from time to time. "Angel didn't mention any clans, but it doesn't mean there isn't one."

The last one to move, Roxy skipped to catch the other two. "Can we stop and check it out? I've never seen a real castle."

Tristan raised a brow. "Not one?"

She shook her head. "Nope. We don't have any where I come from."

"You'll have to satisfy your curiosity from the road, Rox." He hated the deflated expression on her face, but it wasn't the time for sightseeing. "Let's find Etain."

The suggestion seemed to lift her spirits. "Yeah. We should find her first."

Roxy stared at the large, gray stone structure as they passed and would have walked straight into the ravine had Isobel not grabbed her by the arm. "Roxy! Pay attention to where you're going."

"Oh! Gosh! Thanks, Isobel. It's so magnificent."

"I guess with it being your first, it seems that way."

She turned to Isobel with wide eyes. "You've been to a castle?"

"A couple. They were much nicer than this one. If it weren't for the guards at the gate, I'd say it was abandoned."

"They don't look too friendly, do they?"

"Come on, ladies. If you stare too long, they might come asking why."

Roxy walked on but glanced over her shoulder every so often until the castle could no longer be seen.

Not long after, they were rewarded with the sight of a small town and walked into its center. Isobel turned, scoping out the buildings on both sides of the road. "Should we check in the pub and ask if they've seen her? Do you think she came this way?"

Tristan shrugged and pointed toward a line of trees ahead. "Hard to tell. It looks like the forest is that way."

"Would she come into town?" Roxy asked.

"Your guess is as good as mine." Tristan turned to the pub. "It looks to be a nice place. I'll go in and ask."

"We'll come with." Isobel and Roxy followed him inside.

A fair-haired young woman behind the bar smiled at his approach. "Yer a fresh face. Are ya new to these parts?"

Tristan flashed his best smile. "I am. We are." He indicated his traveling companions. "We've come looking for a friend, a young woman. Have you seen anyone with silver hair and blue eyes?"

She dismissed Isobel and Roxy with a faint smile. Turning to Tristan, she beamed again. "I don't recall anyone with silver hair. Let me check with me manager."

"Thank you, milady."

She smirked. "Give me the chance and you'll be changing yer tune." With a wink, she disappeared into a back room.

He smiled, feeling the burn in his cheeks as he turned to his companions and shrugged. Isobel glared with hands on her hips and Roxy raised a brow, crossing her arms over her chest. "It's not like I will."

"No. You won't." Isobel went silent when the girl reappeared.

"Sorry, love. No one here's seen anyone by that description. Have ya tried Murtagh's?" She motioned toward the large front window. "It's across the way."

Tristan and the girls turned at the same time, staring at the dark, mysterious building on the other side of the road. Tristan swallowed and cleared his throat. "Can't say as we have. Ta for checking."

"Wish I could've helped. Come back if yer looking for a hot meal or a brew." She leaned over the counter. "We'll fix ya right up." Her smile was a tempting invitation, lips red as wine, and creamy breasts peeking from her top.

Despite Isobel's slap to the back of his head, he returned the smile. "Gotta go." Once outside the pub, he turned on her. "What the bloody hell was that for? She was being nice."

"Do you really think she finds you special? She probably says it to every guy who walks in there."

"At least she made an effort. It's nice to be appreciated once in a while."

Roxy linked an arm with his. "Aw, Tristian, we appreciate you. We just aren't interested in jumping your bones."

He pulled his arm from hers when she giggled. "I'm headed to the other pub. I doubt Etain would ever go into a place like—"

"Maybe but we have to be certain." Isobel skipped across the road.

Tristan went after her. "Isobel!"

At the door of the mysterious pub, she laughed, opening the door. "I'll be in and out. What's the worst that could happen?"

Roxy ran after him. "Don't worry, Tris. If there's trouble, she'll come out. Give her a chance."

"If there's trouble, she won't have a chance."

She grabbed him by the arm. "You're going to embarrass her."

"What?"

"It didn't take five minutes for the girl over there to tell us Etain hadn't been seen. Give her five, at least."

His breath caught in his throat. The hairs on his head stood on end and his gut rolled. In his experience, places like this were not where you entered alone, especially being new to the area. But he stayed with Roxy. "She has five. No more."

He counted off what he considered to be a total of five minutes in his mind and made a move toward the pub despite Roxy's insistence it had only been three. Just as he stepped into the foyer, Isobel shoved through the interior doors, huffed at his presence, and bypassed him.

"Isobel! What happened?"

With another huff, she stopped and faced him. "They haven't seen her either. I can't believe she hasn't come into town."

"Well, maybe there's another town on the other side of those trees. Let's go that way and see what we find."

The three followed the worn path to the edge of town into the shadows of the trees and spread out but not so far they would lose sight of each other. Deeper into the forest, Tristan motioned to stop. "There's a lot of tracks here."

The girls joined him. Roxy crouched for a closer look. "It doesn't look like a scuffle. Just lots of footprints."

"My thoughts exactly." Tristan eyed the trees in front of them.

"What do you think it means?" Isobel asked, doing her own speculation of the area.

"Who knows with Etain. If it *is* her."

Isobel narrowed her eyes and placed her hands on her hips. "She's here and she's found others."

Tristan snorted. "Or they found her."

"Doesn't matter. She's probably waiting for us to show up."

Roxy scratched her head. "How would she know we're coming?"

"Not us in particular. More like waiting for G to return."

Once again, Tristan led the way. "Let's keep moving. If G shows, I for one do not want to miss our way home."

# NO ONE GOES ALONE

"I say, Etain." One of her more recent acquisitions, Boswell, an older gentleman with sports jacket and trousers, interrupted a martial arts class led by another new Alamir, Lee. "Might I have moment?"

Lee spun out of a high kick, taking the Brit by surprise. "We're in the middle of training. Can't it wait?"

Etain stepped in between the two. "Sorry, Lee. Give me a few minutes. You can continue with Sonia and Khan."

He bowed his head and turned to his other students.

Etain linked an arm with Boswell and led him away from the small group. "What can I do for you, sir?"

"It is more of what I can do for you, miss."

His formality always made her smile. "What's that?"

"I do believe Mr. Kania and the twins have acquired a young man."

Finding a new Alamir was always uplifting. In the past few weeks, she and Kania had found six others, Boswell being the first of the six. "Really? So soon?"

"As I understand it, he is not very accommodating of Mr. Kania's advances."

"Well, he must've done something to provoke Mr. Kania."

"Blood has been spilled."

Etain stopped. "Blood? Holy shit, Boswell. Where are they?"

He grimaced, his cheeks reddening. "Mistress Etain! Language, please. We may be in a wild world—"

"This is serious, Boswell. What does the man look like?"

He straightened his jacket and bow tie. "Light hair, dark cloak. I could not see much more than that."

*Shit! Shit! Shit!*

"Etain. Did you hear me?"

"Hmm? Yes, it's not easy to get details when you're running away." She continued walking on her own.

"That is not very nice, mistress."

She turned, walking backward. "Just being honest, Boswell. You're not a fighter in the physical sense and it's fine. Your tactical knowledge makes up for it. Would you get Lee and the others to join us, please?"

His head high, he turned and proudly walked back toward the others. Etain smiled and headed in the other direction.

"Please don't be Ronan."

Fortunately, Kania and the twins, Cobar and Jarli, had subdued the stranger away from the campsite. At first glance, the outline of the hunched figure didn't seem familiar. But it had been a while since she'd last seen the man.

"Kania, Boswell tells me—"

The captive turned at her voice.

"Tristan?" She rushed to his side as he stood. "Holy shit. What're you doing here?" She gave Kania a stern glance. "Are you okay? Has G returned?"

Kania crossed his arms over his chest and rubbed his jaw. "Don't give me the evil eye, lady. He threw the first punch."

"There's three of you," she retorted, taking in Tristan's split lip and bruised forehead.

"Sorry, Miss Etain," said Cobar, bowing his head.

"He jumped Mr. Kania," added his twin sister, Jarli. "His manners are bad."

Although her back was turned to her people, she grinned at Tristan, drinking in every inch of him. "I'm sorry for my new Alamir, but I'm damned glad to see you."

"Exuberant, aren't they?" Tristan returned her smile. "I think they will do well."

"Are you alone?"

"I am now. Isobel and Roxy came with me, but we lost each other in the forest."

She turned to the twins. "Time to use your tracking skills. Two young women. One has dark hair, blue eyes. The other is a redhead with gold eyes. If you find anyone else, avoid them. Got it?"

"Yes, Ms. Etain," the two said in unison and disappeared into the trees.

"Aussies?"

Etain chuckled. "Aboriginals. Kania is German. You'll meet the rest soon."

"There's more?"

"I've had to keep myself busy somehow. Has G returned?"

"Not that I know of. When we found out you were missing, we came to find you."

She lowered her eyes for a moment, touched by his words. "Thank you, Tristan." Her gaze met his. "It means a lot. Where'd G go?"

"South America."

Her eyes widened briefly. "Hell, at this rate, we'll have an entire clan by the time he comes back, if he bothers. Kania, we're gonna head to the river and get him cleaned up. You're in charge if anything else happens."

"Sure. Thanks for your concern." He picked up a stick as long as he was tall. "I think I'll go help the twins."

Tristan watched the man walk off. "Did I interrupt?"

"Pfft! No. Kania's a good man. You took him by surprise, is all. Let's get you to the river."

"Oh, wait." Tristan grabbed a pack at his feet. "I brought your backpack, sword included."

Etain stared at the pack in his hand, her heart pounding. "I thought I'd never see it again." Tears burned in her eyes taking the pack and threw an arm around his neck, kissing him on the lips. His arms wrapped around her waist, pulling her body to his.

The clearing of a throat opened their eyes. "Do I get a welcome kiss, too?"

They gazed into one another's eyes for a moment. Etain let go, stepped back, and smiled. The pack hit the ground as she whirled around. "Roxy!" Catching the girl in a bear sized hug, she gave her a kiss. Not as intense as with Tristan but it did the job. "Hi!"

Roxy laughed, a blush on her cheeks. "Hi."

"I have missed y'all."

"Um, yeah. We've missed you, too. Has Isobel made it yet?"

Her smile encompassed them both. "Man, I can't believe you're here." She turned to Roxy. "I sent someone out to find you and Isobel. Hopefully, they'll come back with her soon."

Roxy eyed Tristan head to toe. "What happened to you?"

He shrugged, hooking his thumbs in the pockets of his pants, giving her a lazy grin. "A misunderstanding of intent."

"We were headed to the river." Etain grabbed her pack, smiled at Tristan, and linked an arm with Roxy. "I'll introduce you to my newbies afterward."

<br>

Refreshed after a wash at the river, Etain, Roxy, and Tristan returned to the campsite, where most of the others were preparing an evening meal. "Hey, everyone, gather round. I want to introduce you to a couple of friends."

Boswell scanned the faces at the fire. "Where are Kania and the twins?"

"They're searching for one other friend." Etain ran a hand through her hair. "Um, y'all, this is Roxy and Tristan. I met them not too long ago. They've been Alamir longer than any of us."

She stood between the two and nodded at each person as she went around the circle. "Tristan, Roxy, this gentleman to your left is Boswell. He's a tactical genius. Any chance you get to chat with him, please do."

Next came the other women in the group. "Sonia is the tall lady. A smithy and excellent swordswoman. The woman next to her is Khan. She is a mean negotiator." Etain chuckled. "She's not mean, just extremely good at negotiating everything. Be careful with this one."

Khan adjusted her hijab and smiled. "Welcome. We're happy to meet friends of Etain's."

"And this gentleman to your right is Lee. He's from the States and likes to act like he doesn't understand things but don't fall for it. He knows his stuff."

Lee bowed. "You've taken away my fun, Etain. I learn much more about people as a peasant."

She nudged Tristan. "He's been teaching us martial arts. You'll find him helpful with your techniques."

"Oh? Which style are you trained in, Lee?"

"All."

Tristan sputtered and coughed. "All?"

Etain laughed at his response. "He's even created his own form."

Lee raised a brow. "Should you prove proficient in the art, perhaps I will share it with you, young one."

"I would like that, sir. Thank you."

"There's three more. Tristan had the pleasure of meeting them earlier. Kania, and the twins, Jarli and Cobar." She rubbed her hands together. "Is anyone else starving?"

Several heads bobbed in the group, but Khan answered, "Your friends are lucky today. We have fish tonight."

"Can we help?" Tristan asked.

"If you will stoke the fire, you can cook the fish." Khan handed over a basket weaved of plants from the riverside filled with the catch of the day. "Etain, if you will cut the bark into finer pieces, there should be enough for everyone. We have fruit, too."

"You got it." She sat near the fire with a basket of freshly cut bark.

Roxy sat next to her and helped. "Are the three you mentioned the ones who beat up Tristan?"

A flurry of sparks rose from the fire. "They didn't beat me—"

Etain interrupted his heated retort. "It was a misunderstanding on both parts. He gave as good as he got."

Roxy eyed Tristan with furrowed brows but they lifted when she looked at Etain. "What else do they do besides misunderstand strangers?"

"Kania was an architect, but likes carpentry, and whittles a mean stick."

Her gaze roamed over the group. "Looks like he's been busy. What about the other two?"

"They're the youngest but killer at tracking."

Tristan kneeled by the fire, speared the gutted fish, and propped it over the fire. "Any powers?"

Etain pushed the hair from her face with the back of her hand and cut into a piece of bark. "Nothing's manifested yet but it's only been a few weeks."

He kept his eyes on the main course as he spoke, "In our experience, they usually require an extreme circumstance to show."

"It's been quiet." No way was she telling how Kania found her.

"Good," Roxy said. "I'm sure it's helped them get used to this new life."

Etain dumped her pieces of bark into the basket with Roxy's bits. "I hope so."

"Did something happen?" Tristan asked.

She grabbed a few of the larger pieces and spread them on the flat stone in front of her, focusing more on how they were positioned than cutting into smaller pieces.

When she didn't respond, he turned. "Etain? What happened?"

If she met his gaze, the whole debacle with Ronan would spill out. What would they think? Allowing herself to be deceived and cornered and running away like a fool. It felt like running was all she'd done since coming to the Alamir.

Roxy stopped slicing and lowered her voice. "Don't be afraid. No one else needs to know."

Etain lowered her head. *Suck it up. Tell them everything. Ronan could return—*

Hearing exclamations from the others, she lifted her head. Kania, Jarli, and Cobar came into the camp and headed straight toward her. Something was wrong. She saw it in the way they moved. When the firelight shone on Kania's face, she stood.

"What is it?"

Jarli spoke first. "We didn't find her."

Followed by her brother. "But we saw footprints. Lots of footprints."

Her gaze went to the tall German, who stared at her with hard eyes and pursed lips. "We could not find them, Etain."

Tristan and Roxy came to their feet. "Who?" Roxy asked.

Kania eyed her from head to toe. "I take it you're the dark-haired one." His angry gaze returned to Etain. "Then it's the redhead who's in trouble."

"How do you know?" Tristan asked, reaching for his sword.

"Like Cobar said, there's lots of prints. Humans and horses. We trailed them to the edge of the forest but stopped there. From what we saw, the prints went south."

Tristan belted the straps of his scabbard across his chest. "Why didn't you go further?"

Etain blew out a breath, running a hand through her hair. "Because I've told them not to leave the forest."

Jarli seemed to understand. "Is it *Bok*?"

Etain held the young woman's blue-eyed gaze with her own. "I don't know, Jarli."

Tristan laid a hand on Etain's shoulder. "Are *they* what happened?"

"We have to find Isobel."

"What's south of here, Etain?" Kania asked.

She sheathed her dagger in her boot and grabbed her sword from the pack. "A town."

"And a castle." Roxy added.

Etain stopped and turned. "You came past the castle and through town?" At her nod, she approached her. "Did anything happen?"

Roxy shrugged. "We walked past the castle."

"Did anyone see you?"

"No. We didn't see anyone."

Etain pressed her lips together. "What happened in town?"

Tristan's voice made her turn again. "Not much. We checked the local pubs and asked the bartenders if they'd seen you."

"You didn't talk to anyone else?"

"No, just the bartenders."

"Wait," Roxy said. "We all went into the one pub, but Isobel went alone to the other."

Etain grabbed her by the arm. "Which one?"

"W-What?"

"Did she go into the light pub or the dark? It's important, Roxy." At her blank look, Etain sucked in a breath and closed her eyes, forcing herself to relax. Her eyes opened as she breathed out and let go of the girl. "I'm sorry. One pub is bright and light with lots of windows. The other has windows but they're blacked out or so dirty they look black. It's not a place to go into by yourself. Especially someone like Isobel."

"I knew it!" Tristan huffed. "I told her we'd go in together. But she insisted."

Etain turned to him. "Are you sure she only spoke to the bartender?"

"She said she went straight to the bar. The bartender was useless, so she left. Angel said you were in a forest, so we walked to the trees."

Etain paced away. *Could he have been there? A strange redhead would certainly pique his interest. Footprints mean he wasn't alone.* She shook her head, biting her bottom lip. *Why didn't I see the coward in him from the start?* Eyes narrowed and shoulders straight, she paced back to the group. "I have to go."

Kania stepped in front of her with a twin on either side, blocking her within their half-circle. "Everyone goes."

"No! I won't be responsible for any of you getting hurt."

Khan came forward, speaking in her sensical, straightforward way. "You did not make us Alamir, Etain. Despite how you feel, you are not responsible for any one of us. But you have taken on the responsibility of teaching us what it means to be Alamir. If we do not do this today, when? Will there ever be a better day to step into our Alamir lives? A day when we can fight against the very thing we were created for and help someone in need?"

Sonia stepped forward, her Bō at her side. "We have learned our lessons well. We are ready."

Their earnest faces pierced her heart. Her stomach fluttered with a thousand, black winged creatures, making her want to scream. Who was she to judge their abilities? To tell them they weren't ready? She'd done her best to help them in their transitions so they would never feel the fear she'd experienced every day since her parents and brother died.

"Damn, Khan. I can't imagine anything more powerful than a logical woman."

At her admitted resolution, Kania and the twins stepped back. Khan smirked and bowed her head. "We are with you."

"Boswell, stay here in the off-chance Isobel shows. She's a beautiful redhead with gold eyes."

His initial frown dissolved into a smile as he adjusted his bow tie. "I will not let you down, milady."

"Kania, Lee, and Sonia, you're with me. Here, Sonia, take my sword. You will wield it a lot better than me."

The Amazon of a woman accepted the weapon. "It is smaller than I am used to, but I will do it justice."

"Cobar, Jarli, and Khan, you'll go to the opposite end of town and keep watch. Do not engage with anyone, especially if they come from the dark pub. You're to observe and report only."

She sensed the brewing volcano behind her and faced Tristan's hard eyes and clenched jaws. "Do I really have to say it? You and Roxy are with me."

"Where are we going?"

"The castle. Let's go."

*Not yet*, came a voice in her head, speaking in the rhythm of her heart. *You haven't told them of what they face.*

The expressions in front of her seemed to understand the seriousness of what was to come. *But do they? Really? You say you feel responsible, but you aren't acting in the manner of a responsible leader. Put aside your pride. Tell them what has happened, so they are prepared for the treachery ahead.*

"I have to tell you something," came from her mouth without another thought.

Brows furrowed, shoulders tensed, and storms brewed in their eyes.

Etain licked her lips and braced herself. "Do not trust anyone except your own people. The people we face might try to fool you by saying they're Alamir. Perhaps in the beginning, but not anymore. They work with the *Bok*."

Tristan's eyes presented the most turbulence, changing from their sea blue to gray to black. "How do you know?"

*Just spit it out.* "Not long after I arrived, I discovered the town and met who I thought was a fellow Alamir. I mean, he had to be, right? We're in the Alamir realm. Who else would be living here?"

Cobar reminded her. "The *Bok*."

"Yes, yes, but at the time, I was alone, in a foreign place, and wasn't thinking straight. His friendly persona gave me a sense of comfort. Like he would watch out for me. He was...is handsome and charming. He even offered to help me gather new Alamir and match them with clans needing to grow." Her gaze went to each of her people. "They treat you right until you're in their clutches. Then you're locked away and brutalized until the *Bok* take over, provided you aren't *too* broken. I did not see the coward in him. But I do now."

Jarli looked ready to cry. "What is 'too broken'?"

"I think it differs depending on the person. Fortunately, for me, it didn't get that far." The thought of any of her people at Ronan's mercy brought tears to her eyes. "So be careful. All of you. No one goes alone."

# LONG SHOT

At the edge of the forest, memories of the first time she left its shadows haunted her. Searching for what? Help? Company? Safety?

Khan stood next to her. "What do you see, Etain?"

She breathed out with a "Hmph." But found only deceit, greed, and disregard for others. "Stay on the path. It'll take you right into town. Do *not* veer from the path until you're on the other side. Then it's your job to remain unseen but see everything."

The twins headed along the path.

Etain turned to Khan. "If we aren't out of the castle by daylight, you and the twins head back to Boswell at camp. Don't come after us."

Khan clasped her hands in front of her. "What do we do then, Etain?"

"Be vigilant and watch for strangers. If anyone approaches you, ask for Angel. The good Alamir will know who she is. The bad ones won't."

"I understand." She touched Etain's shoulder. "Be safe, milady."

"You, too. See you soon." Khan disappeared into the darkness.

"Etain," Tristan stepped to her side. "I suggest we split. A group of strangers will raise concerns."

"You're right. What if we go two at a time each walking opposite the other just off the path? Should anyone show, which I doubt anyone will at this time of night, it'll be easier to disappear."

"And when we get to town?" Lee asked.

"The light pub will be to your left about midway down. A walkway next to it leads to a street behind the pub. I'm not sure, but I think it goes for a couple of blocks where you'll find a small path that takes you back to the main road."

Lee exchanged a glance with Kania. "We will go first. If there is trouble, we can deal with it."

"Okay. Good idea—"

Roxy and Sonia came forward. "We'll go next and serve as their back-up should it be needed. Plus, where Sonia has sheer size, I have exceptional balance and reflexes. While she walks the earth, I'll dance on top of the buildings." She shrugged. "More or less."

Her news brought a smile to Etain's lips, yet she couldn't shake a sense of betrayal that Roxy hadn't mentioned her new power. "Incredible! When did that happen?"

"I'm not sure. I think it's been developing since we left the complex. I didn't want to say anything until I felt more comfortable with it."

"Trust yourself and be careful."

Kania headed down the path, large stick in hand. Lee followed from the side of the road, darting from tree to rock to bush.

Standing behind the girls, Etain nudged Tristan, and whispered, "Anything new with you?"

A mischievous glint shone in his eyes. "Aside from trying to steel another kiss from our leader, I've not much to add."

An uncertain "hmph" sounded in her throat accompanied by a daring flash of cockiness. "We get through this; you can have two."

The bravado of her words wiped the grin from his face. "What?"

Etain joined Sonia and Roxy. "We won't be far behind."

Roxy glanced over her shoulder and chuckled. "I don't know what you said but you need to fix him. He looks pretty worthless."

"He'll be fine. Y'all be safe."

Sonia bowed her head. "We will see you soon."

Tristan and Etain watched the two move along either side of the road. "Will you tell me what happened with this Ronan?"

"Nothing. He didn't do a damn thing."

"I see. Were you hurt?"

She crossed her arms over her chest. "Mainly my pride but it could've been much worse."

"If he didn't help, how did you get away?"

"An electric charge. From my hand to a cretin's balls."

Tristan cringed. "Ouch. Did Ronan try to stop you?"

"Hard to say. One minute I'm frying a toad's bangers and the next I'm standing outside the castle in the rain. I ran to town and stayed in a room at the pub."

"Wait a minute. Where'd you get the money?"

"It was late. No one was around and the keys were there. I slipped out the next day and been in the forest ever since."

Tristan ran both hands through his shaggy blond mane. "That's a lot. You've lost weight but you don't look starved. How is it you and the others have survived?"

"You saw it. Bark, fruit, and sometimes fish. There's all sorts of food in the forest."

He gave her a lopsided grin. "Is that one of your Alamir powers?"

"Ha. Funny. No. We used to camp when I was a kid."

"You've never mentioned your family. How did they take your transition?"

Her heart stopped. She curled her hands into fists to keep the overwhelming sadness at bay, but her voice did not waver. "It absolutely killed them. I don't see the girls. We better get going. I'll take the left side."

His gaze burned through the armor she'd built around herself. No one was worth the pain it caused to speak of her family. Although Tristan meant a lot to her, he was not her person. The one who set her soul on fire and filled her heart with so much love she could hardly breathe. Once she avenged their deaths, maybe she could open up to someone and share the horrible story.

*Stop daydreaming. This isn't a fairytale, and I'm not a princess. The only one who's gonna save me is me.*

Somewhere along her way to town, Etain lost track of Tristan. Rather than search for him, she swung past the light pub and detoured to the back street so no one would see her, confident he wasn't far behind. Coming to the main road again, she didn't see the twins or Khan and hoped they were safe.

On the other side of the town, she stood in the middle of the road and faced south.

*Are you ready to do what needs doing?*

*Whatever it takes to keep my friends, new and old, safe. Yes. I am ready.*

*Is your fire ready?*

Etain held her hands in front of her and imagined firelit fingertips. Blue fire ignited across her fingers.

*Good. Use your intuition to suss out the innocents, if there are any. Do not hurt them. Only the evil ones.*

*Like Ronan and the old man?*

*Aye. Like them. Now. Shall we test your other power?*

*Other?*

*The one you used on the old man.*

Much like how she had summoned the fire, she imagined electricity crackling from her hands.

Nothing appeared.

She tried again.

Nothing.

*Maybe it was a one-time thing.*

*No. It is a part of you. Within you. It will come when you need it most.*

*Well, if it doesn't, I have my dagger.*

*It will not fail you.*

"Psssst!"

Etain dropped her hands.

"Psssssssssst! Etain."

She stood still but her eyes scanned the perimeter. A movement to her side made her turn. "Kania?"

"Hurry! Come over here."

She joined him in a cropping of rocks. "What're you doing?"

He pulled her deeper into the formation. "What are *you* doing? People can see you."

"There isn't anyone around."

"You might want to look a little closer. We think the whole clan is in attendance."

She edged to the end of a large rock and peeked around the corner. Darkness surrounded the castle, but she noticed movement at the entrance of the bridge to the main gates. As her eyes adjusted, she saw others along the upper walkway and inched back. "I didn't know there were so many in the clan. There aren't enough of us. I can't—"

"Your friend is in there."

"Maybe the others aren't aware of what he's doing."

"If she's in that castle, they're aware. Why else would they be on alert?"

"How do you know?"

"Something Roxy said when they passed earlier. They didn't see anyone and now, when your friend is missing, the place is crawling."

"Yeah. The night I was there, I didn't see anyone except Ronan and his creepy friend."

"They underestimated you."

She ran a hand through her hair. "They won't this time."

Kania took hold of her upper arms, forcing her to look at him. "You have to make them underestimate you again."

"What do you expect me to do?"

"Take the lead. We'll have your back."

She broke free of his grip. "I can't lead us into that! Everyone thinks they're ready but not even I'm ready."

"Boswell's been teaching us tactics here and there. We've all been learning from each other. If three-hundred Spartans can push back a Persian army, we can take on these—"

"Not for long. I'd like all of us to share another day together."

Kania shrugged. "We have something they didn't have."

"What's that?"

"You."

She pressed her palms against her eyes, afraid her head would explode. "Have you lost your mind?" She dragged her fingers down her face and glared at him. "I just said—"

"We haven't discovered our powers, but you have. I've seen what you can do."

Shaking her head, she held up a hand. "Stop. Burning a bunch of ivy doesn't compare—"

"And David only had a sling shot."

"Are you a preacher now?"

He moved closer and grinned in her face. "Complete with brimstone and my beautiful blue ecclesiastical fire."

"Ronan saw what I did to the creep."

Kania pulled back with a raised brow. "I don't think he saw what you think he saw. Otherwise, I doubt he would've made this move."

"Well, that's the thing, some people aro too stupid to know their stupid." She turned away from him. "Despite the power he saw, selling me to the *Bok* could be a big payoff for him."

"Why give your enemy a powerful advantage? If that's his plan, it's our responsibility to put him out of his misery. He's too stupid to live."

She shrugged. "Okay, well, maybe he thinks I'm gullible enough to believe anything he says and that together we can rule the Alamir and defeat the *Bok*."

"There's only one way to find out."

"Yes, yes. I must go in." *Such a simple solution.* She paced back and forth, deep in thought, rubbing a finger over her lips.

Kania huffed. "Not by—"

She waved a hand as she paced. "No."

"No? Have you forgotten—"

"No. You will go with me."

"Me?"

She stopped, bowed her head, and fisted her hands, but her eyes met his. "The five of us will go in."

Kania paced this time. "We need Tristan."

"No, we don't. Ronan and I will pick up where we left off."

The wildness in his eyes left no doubts of his thoughts. "Where was that?"

"I bring him new Alamir, and he matches them with needy clans."

"Sacrificial lambs to the slaughter?"

Lee, Sonia, and Roxy joined them. "Sacrificial lambs?" Roxy echoed.

Etain's plan glowed in her mind. "It'll play perfectly to Ronan's ego."

Lee crossed his arms over his chest. "You said you parted on bad terms."

"If I act like I've been following the plan all along and y'all act like you don't know much about anything, it won't matter. He's about the profit."

Sonia leaned against the solid rock. "So we go in together. How do we get out together?"

"It'll take some time. I figure he'll lock you in a room or something. Isobel included. He'll need time to contact the *Bok*. While he's doing that, I'll break you out during the night and we escape."

"What if they split us up?" Roxy asked.

"Why would they? It'll be easier to keep you in the same area."

"Maybe in your head," she placed her hands on her hips, "but they might prefer to separate us. Keep us in the dark until we're sold."

Kania stroked his mustache in thought. "How will our escape make any difference if we don't stop him and his clan from selling others?"

Etain ran a hand through her hair. "Oh my God, I don't know! We don't have time to consider every angle. We have to get Isobel out of there and pray we aren't already too late."

"What about Khan and the twins?" Lee asked.

"They go back to camp and wait for G."

Kania exchanged looks with Lee and Sonia. "G?"

Etain bit her bottom lip. "Did I not mention G?"

"No," Sonia said, shifting from one hip to the other.

"Man." She rolled her eyes. "Sorry, y'all. G is one of the goods guys. He helps new Alamir. That's where I got the idea from."

Kania cocked his head. "Why would he come to this place?"

Roxy approached Etain with an apology in her eyes and turned to the others. "Because of you...and us. We were like you not long ago. He found us and helped us transition."

Lee glanced at Kania. "If he left you here, why would he come back?"

Kania was right about Ronan and his clan. In the way off-chance they could make their escape with Isobel in tow, it wouldn't fix the larger problem of the abuse and trafficking of other Alamir to the *Bok*. "Let's get Isobel and us away from this place first. With any luck, Master G'll show up and take care of the rest."

Kania eyed the small group. "It's a long shot but I like it. What about the rest of you?"

The three answered in unison. "We're in."

# TAKE NO PRISONERS

The guards snapped to attention at their approach. One pressed a finger to his ear and mumbled from the side of his mouth.

Etain held her head high and didn't waste her breath on the two, leading her small band through the entrance and across the bridge. The next two guards opened the main doors, the metal screeching as though in pain, and moved aside.

The large foyer brought back her first night in the castle. The cold, gray walls and minimal décor had accomplished what they'd been created to do—intimidate. Tonight, a friend needed her help. Nothing about this place would intimidate her again. Neither would Ronan or his clan.

A young woman came to escort them into a cavernous room of the same gray stonework and decorated with the occasional drab tapestry that did nothing to quell the cold. The lack of furniture made her wonder about the use of the room. A large fireplace mocked her with its cold, dark façade.

On the other side of the space stood Ronan and those she assumed were his clan. A few steps to his side, the old man who had assaulted her held a dagger aimed at the only warmth in the room—Isobel. Her golden eyes lit in a fiery glow. Her rich, red hair danced about her face as she shook her head. "No!"

At the snap of Ronan's fingers, the old man silenced her with the same grimy hand he'd used on her. Kania, standing behind Etain, pressed his leg to hers ever so slightly and whispered, "Steady."

She sucked in a long, slow breath, her jaws clenched. Her hand twitched with the desire to stab both Ronan and the cretin in the throat with her dagger.

The initial surprise in Ronan's eyes degraded into smugness. "So, ya *are* alive, after all."

As she released the breath, her shoulders lowered, and a sense of peace came over her. The game must be played perfectly if she, Isobel, and the others were to walk out with their lives. She licked her lips and gave him an easy smile. "Of course, I am. I've been busy finding new Alamir." She waved a carefree hand toward those around her. "As you can see. What did you think I was doing?"

Her cheerful response wiped the smugness from his face. He cleared his throat and shifted on his feet. "I-I haven't seen you in weeks."

"As I said, I've been busy." She didn't dare look at Isobel again for fear of losing her resolve. Focused on Ronan, she noticed differences in his appearance. His face seemed haggard; the lines deeper than when she first met him. As a matter of fact, he no longer struck her as handsome and any charm she thought he'd had was gone. *Quite satisfying, in my opinion.*

"Thank you for helping my latest find. Directions are not her forte. We thought she was lost." When he didn't respond, she raised a brow. "We *are* still partners, aren't we? I bring them in, and you find them a clan. Right?"

The man touched his cheek as though he'd been slapped. His eyes cleared and was with her again. "Right. I have a clan in mind."

Etain softened her face and imagined the biggest puppy dog eyes she could, hoping they would project through hers. "You do?" She clapped her hands and grinned at those around her. "Did you hear that? You can all go together!"

*Bless their souls.* The four smiled at the same time and exchanged hugs.

Roxy kissed her on one cheek. "Etain, you're the best. Thank you so much. You were right when you said he was an angel." When she kissed the other, she whispered, "Demon angel."

The weight on her shoulders lifted despite the ugly glint in Ronan's eyes and the sneer he shared with the cretin.

"I'll be needing time to get in touch with the chieftain and make arrangements. Ya can stay with us until everything is set. Guards!"

A team of six appeared in the doorway and approached the small group, splitting Etain from the others.

"I'll stay with them."

Ronan approached her, the smug smile on his face. "Etain. It's best to say goodbye here. We need them ready to travel at a moment's notice."

A yelp from Isobel's direction made her turn. "Etain! Don't let them leave—"

"Shaddup, ya wench." The cretin yanked her head back and sneered. "Don't fuck this up."

Etain struggled to keep her naïve façade as Ronan laughed in her face. *There it is. How did I mistake your arrogance for charm?* "Ronan? What's going on?"

He loomed over her, running a strand of her silver hair through his fingers. "*You* are not going anywhere with them. *You're* staying here with me." His gaze flicked to Isobel. "And *her*."

"Why?"

"Seeing you explains why no new meat was coming to town. You, my lovely Etain, did exactly what you said you would do, and going forward, you will do it for me. For my clan."

She stepped back. "Do it *for* you?"

"We were ready to disband and scatter to the ends of the earth, but here you are, offering us a lifeline, a steady stream of income."

He grabbed her arm and pulled her close, his lips hovering at her ear. "You bring 'em in, me darlin', and we'll find 'em a home."

She tried to jerk away but his viselike grip held her fast. "Why keep her here? Let her go with them."

"Ya must think me a right fool." His gaze pierced into hers. "She's me insurance you stay put and keep us in the manner we've come accustomed to. Me little breadwinner."

*Man, how I would love to vomit in your face. Keep cool, Etain. Don't spiral out of control or he'll have you both. Call his bluff.* "You'd be better off selling her. One less mouth to feed."

"We'll not be selling the only thing to keep you working." Her skin crawled when he laughed. "If ya give us any trouble, she'll be the one to pay. We'll get plenty for the lot you've brought, along with the three in town. The young ones'll bring a pretty price. The *Bok* treat their sex slaves better than the fighters."

*Khan. Jarli and Cobar. Shit!*

His laugh grated on her last nerve.

"If you touch anyone, I will kill you."

Ronan snapped a finger. "Tenant, show her."

Her head ached from the blood rush pumping through her as the cretin raised his dagger over Isobel's chest. It no longer mattered what this asshole said. She would agree to anything to save her life. As long as she lived, they could figure it out together. Etain twisted out of his grip. "Stop!"

The dagger halted in its descent. Captivated by Isobel's golden gaze, Etain didn't understand what the woman was trying to convey. Not until her hands wrapped around the hilt of the dagger and plunged it into her heart.

"No, Isobel!" Etain screamed, shoving Ronan away and running toward her, watching her collapse in slow motion, taking the old man down with her.

Etain slid to her knees and laid her hands over Isobel's, blood seeping from the wound. "No. No. No! Isobel! Why?" She glared at the old man through her tears, her anger growing with every breath.

He shoved Isobel into her, scrambling to escape her wrath, but Etain moved faster than he ever would, dragged the dagger from her boot and lunged, stabbing him in the thigh and twisting the blade. The old man screamed.

Etain crawled over Isobel and up the length of the old man aware that others of his clan moved toward her. Blood gushed when she yanked the dagger from the wound and stood over him. Blue electrical charges snapped and crackled around her from head to toe. Her dagger in hand, she swung her arm in an arc and released an electrical rope, slicing the charging men in half.

Other clan members screamed, pushing and shoving each other to put distance between them and the firebrand. Etain didn't care about them. She pivoted in the old man's blood in search of Ronan. Not finding him, her gaze went to her friends surrounded by the guards.

Kania lifted his stick and brought it crashing down on the heads of the ones in front of him. Lee laid into two more with his special brand of martial arts. Sonia and Roxy brought their swords round but those clan members who could, ran for their lives.

By the time she returned to Isobel, it was too late. Her once beautiful golden eyes were glazed in a dead stare. Tears trickled over her cheeks as she hugged the young woman to her and whispered, "Isobel. I'm so sorry. I'm so sorry." She pulled back, staring into her dead eyes and kissed her on the lips. "We're going home to G, beautiful girl. Go with the others for now and I'll be with you soon."

Etain's small group rallied around her, protecting her as she lifted Isobel in her arms, and walked together toward the main doors. Once on the other side, Etain surrendered Isobel to Kania. "Get across the bridge and away from this place. I'll catch up."

His eyes were as sad as her heart. "Etain, come with us."

She held his gaze, fighting the desire to gaze on Isobel's beautiful face frozen in death's repose. *We were almost free.* "Have you seen Ronan?"

Roxy squeezed past Kania. "He ran into one of the hallways." She grabbed her bloody hand and squeezed. "Please don't go back in there. I can't bear to mourn another friend."

Etain stepped beyond her reach and turned to the metal doors, swallowing her grief. *No time for tears. I caused this. I have to fix it.* "Go. I'll be along shortly."

Once the sound of their footsteps faded, she sucked in a breath, swiped her eyes, and entered the castle but turned toward the stairs. The feel of the smooth wooden handrail against her hand offered a strange sense of peace. Biding her time, she slowed her pace as she ascended to the second floor thinking of her first visit.

An innocent beginning that, in her expectations, had promised to be a fruitful friendship, at its best, and if not, an association. Either way, she'd given her trust to a man who neither deserved nor appreciated it. A man who had no regard for decency. Or innocence. Other than to take advantage of both and twist them to fulfill his own desires.

The realizations strengthened her resolve to finish what Ronan had started. He didn't know it yet, but whatever plans he had for the future were about to go up in smoke.

The rubber soles of her boots squeaked on the stone floor. *Good. I want him to hear his end coming.* She followed the hallway to her right and walked to the last set of doors. Large, white, and deceptive. *How impressive they were that night. How naïve was I?* Today, they struck her as more of an oversized tombstone.

She found him where she expected him to be. He turned to her as she approached, mesmerized by the electrical ribbons of blue crackling and sparking around her form.

"We are more alike than you think, Etain. We could rule the world."

She caressed him from shoulder to wrist and intertwined her fingers with his as though they were lovers come together for a final tryst. "Greed is what inspires you to do what you do. What inspires me is love."

His smirk strengthened her convictions. "To the destruction of others?"

"*You* are the destroyer. *I* am the protector."

He shrugged. "*Ar nós seo ar nós sin* (Like this like that)."

She did not smile. She did not shed a tear. His actions spoke louder than the unfamiliar words he spoke. Her broken heart pulsed in time with her ribbons of light, draining the life from his.

No one came to stop her. No one challenged her on her way down the stairs or when she walked through the castle setting everything alight with her blue fire. No one ran to the main doors as she closed them one at a time and welded them to their metal frame from top to bottom.

The screams of her enemies escorted her across the bridge, each footstep leaving a blue flamed print. Freed from their servitude, the ashes of the planks swirled in the breeze. A smile touched her lips as she turned and admired a job well done. "You will never hurt another person. Ever."

Her knees buckled, exhausted by her extreme outlay of power and overcome by the audacity of her actions. *Isobel, you brave, courageous woman. I'm so sorry.* She covered her face with her hands.

In the midst of her weakened state, she sensed a difference within herself. Or perhaps it was more a realization of what she was capable of. What she had always been capable of. An ability unleashed by her transformation into Alamir and intensified by everything that had happened since, bringing her to the acceptance of her Alamir self.

The fire was no longer a challenge. Neither was setting a lying, two-faced bastard alight. Or his dark, dirty castle. The power pulsing beneath her skin extinguished the nagging awkwardness and revealed her path within the Alamir.

"There's no going home. No looking back."

Flames roared through the structure, burning the cancer from inside out, tiny sparks rising to the heavens like faeries dancing in the rain. The raindrops cooled her brow and felt like a thousand tiny pats on the back.

Amid the imagined reassurances, another voice spoke to her. Always last to the party but the loudest among them all. Doubt.

*How many innocents do you think died today because of you?*

*None. No one did a thing to help us or Isobel.*

*Perhaps they had their own Isobels held hostage by the man and his cronies, waiting for their moment to set them free. Maybe the screams you heard belonged to them instead of the clan.*

*No. Ronan wasn't one to wait.*

*He waited for you.*

She bit her bottom lip, running a hand through her hair. *Shut up.*

*You call yourself the protector. What a laugh. You probably destroyed more lives than Ronan ever did in all his time—*

A weight on her shoulder silenced the voice. She turned her head and stared at a face she couldn't put into perspective. He looked familiar. The green-blue eyes and close-cropped sandy hair belonged to another time.

"You'll never know for sure."

When he spoke, the pieces came together. In a way.

"Master G? I-I don't understand."

He offered his hand. "Evil surrounds itself with innocents. Uses them as shields and for their propaganda. There may have been innocents. Or maybe not."

Steadied by his arm around her, she blinked several times. "How did you—"

"Your face tells me everything. It's one of the many things we need to work on."

She rolled her eyes, pressing her lips together.

"Are you able to stand on your own?"

Her knees wobbled but she nodded.

He turned to the burning castle. "I suppose this is your work." She thought she noted a hint of appreciation in his voice. "If innocents were present, what you must remember is that you didn't put them there." He came back to her. "And it wasn't you who put Isobel there either. No." His hand rose to silence her. "I should not have allowed her, Tristan, or Roxy to go."

"How could you have known—"

"We learned of Ronan and his rogue clan some time ago. It's why we visit here on a regular basis."

Her cheeks burned with a sudden heat. "Why didn't *you* stop him?"

His gaze hardened and jaws clenched but soon passed. "I'm not here to govern the Alamir. That responsibility belongs to the Ambassadors. I—We help where we're the most effective."

"Getting rid of clans like his *would* be the most effective—"

"Where would it stop, Etain?" His leathered armor rustled, clasping his hands together in front of him. "At what point would they consider me and my clan the problem and come after us? We stick to what we do best. Let the Alamir take care of their rotten apples."

She furrowed her brows. "You talk like you're not—"

Master G dropped his arms and wiped the rain from his face. "Shall we get out of here?"

"Wait. How did you know where I was? About Isobel?"

"Kania and the others. They should be in the complex."

"So you've met them? And Tristan? I lost him on the way."

"Yes, Tristan. Quite the leader he's proven to be." Master G clasped his hands behind his back. "He searched out the chieftain of the other clan in the area and together they routed the remnants of Ronan's clan. Perhaps you'll find some solace knowing they will be held accountable."

"Perhaps. You mentioned the complex. Is it in the forest?"

He shrugged with a mischievous smirk. "Possibly."

"What about Isobel?"

"She's in Angel's care now. She will be missed. We'll have a ceremony to mourn her passing."

"Thank you." Etain chewed the inside of her lip and looked away, afraid to ask her next question but more afraid not to. "And me?" She slipped her hands into her back pockets and met his steady gaze. "What about me?"

"Yes, what about you?" His arms crossed over his chest as his gaze skimmed over her. "Good question. Shall we save that conversation for later? You need to rest and I need to get out of this blasted rain."

Not the answer she wanted but maybe it was a good thing. Her knees buckled at the first step. Master G's quick reflexes saved her from an unscheduled mud facial.

"Let's take it slow. You've expended a lot of energy today. It'll take time to regain your strength."

"Will it always be like this?"

"Not if I have anything to do with it."

Soaked to the bone, the two walked together along a road lined with people she'd not noticed. Her stomach flipped, aware she was in no shape for another fight, and leaned closer to Master G. "What're they doing? I won't be much help if they—"

He laughed as he eyed the onlookers. "They're here because of you, my lady Etain."

From somewhere behind her, the faint sound of clapping hands grew into a crescendo of appreciation, every face smiling as she passed. Mutterings of *"Go raibh maith agat"* mixed with *"Beannacht leat, a leanbh dao"* washed over her.

"What're they saying, Master G?"

"They're showing appreciation for a brave warrior."

"Brave? Ha. I was scared shitless the entire time."

"Didn't slow you down for a second."

A young couple stepped from the crowd, the woman draping a cloak over Etain while the man slung one over Master G. Securing the cloaks in place, Etain admitted to herself that his presence gave her a sense of comfort. Something she'd not felt in a long time.

"Do we have to walk the whole way?" she asked once they cleared the town. He stopped and gave her a wink, giving her reason to step back. "You're not going to throw me over your shoulder, are you?"

The big man laughed and scooped her into his arms. "Not this time."

In a whirl of light, they appeared in front of the complex. No building ever looked as beautiful as this one in this moment. *I'll never call you a monstrosity again.*

"Shall I carry you in or can you walk?"

"As long as you walk beside me, I think I can."

"So be it."

On her feet, she linked arms with Master G and walked into the next chapter of her Alamir life.

# ALSO BY

**INTO THE KAOS TRILOGY**
CROSSFIRE
KEY OF G
ONCE UPON A DARKNIGHT

**THE BLOOD OF KAOS SERIES**
ALAMIR
DREAMREAPER
FLESH AND BONE
TABOO

# NOTE FROM NESA

Thank you for reading my book(s)!
Whether you love them or hate them,
please share your experience with other readers
and tell them of your journey Into the Kaos.

# ABOUT THE AUTHOR

After marrying her special someone, Nesa decided life was too short to spend it all in one place. Instead of him moving to Texas (her home), she moved to England (his home). Since then, life has been an adventure!

Nesa is a 'learn as you go' kind of gal, which can be challenging, especially when it comes to writing. Although it took a backseat to raising her three children and work, the desire to write never died. Now that her kids are grown, she can indulge in her fantastical stories.

You can find Nesa Miller here:
https://ladyofkaos.com/
FACEBOOK – Nesa Miller
AMAZON – Nesa Miller
TIKTOK – Lady of Kaos

# ACKNOWLEDGEMENTS

A SPECIAL THANK YOU TO

Daniel, my incredible husband – I adore you!

Amy Briggs – Editor Extraordinaire

Amy Queau – Q Designs – Cover Artiste Magnifique

Daniel Palfrey – Talented Artiste

Jennifer Khan – Sassy SEO Marketeuer

# CAN I JUST SAY

Many years ago, a small group came together
in the spirit of community.
They called themselves superheroes.
Super they were and super they remain.
Thank you for your super ways, support,
and continued friendships.

Long live all you Superdudes!